HOW TO GET FILTHY RICH
IN RISING ASIA

HOW TO GET FILTHY RICH IN RISING ASIA

MOHSIN HAMID

HAMISH HAMILTON
an imprint of
PENGUIN BOOKS

HAMISH HAMILTON

Published by the Penguin Group
Penguin Books Ltd, 80 Strand, London WC2R 0RL, England
Penguin Group (USA) Inc., 375 Hudson Street, New York, New York 10014, USA
Penguin Group (Canada), 90 Eglinton Avenue East, Suite 700, Toronto, Ontario, Canada M4P 2Y3
(a division of Pearson Penguin Canada Inc.)
Penguin Ireland, 25 St Stephen's Green, Dublin 2, Ireland (a division of Penguin Books Ltd)
Penguin Group (Australia), 707 Collins Street, Melbourne, Victoria 3008, Australia
(a division of Pearson Australia Group Pty Ltd)
Penguin Books India Pvt Ltd, 11 Community Centre, Panchsheel Park, New Delhi – 110 017, India
Penguin Group (NZ), 67 Apollo Drive, Rosedale, Auckland 0632, New Zealand
(a division of Pearson New Zealand Ltd)
Penguin Books (South Africa) (Pty) Ltd, Block D, Rosebank Office Park,
181 Jan Smuts Avenue, Parktown North, Gauteng 2193, South Africa

Penguin Books Ltd, Registered Offices: 80 Strand, London WC2R 0RL, England

www.penguin.com

First published in the United States of America by Riverhead Books,
a member of Penguin Group (USA) Inc. 2013
First published in Great Britain by Hamish Hamilton 2013
003

Printed in Great Britain by Clays Ltd, St Ives plc

A CIP catalogue record for this book is available from the British Library

HARDBACK ISBN: 978-0-241-14466-4
TRADE PAPERBACK ISBN: 978-0-241-14590-6

www.greenpenguin.co.uk

MIX
Paper from
responsible sources
FSC
www.fsc.org   FSC™ C018179

Penguin Books is committed to a sustainable
future for our business, our readers and our planet.
This book is made from Forest Stewardship
Council™ certified paper.

ALWAYS LEARNING   **PEARSON**

FOR ZAHRA

HOW TO GET FILTHY RICH
IN RISING ASIA

ONE

MOVE TO THE CITY

LOOK, UNLESS YOU'RE WRITING ONE, A SELF-HELP book is an oxymoron. You read a self-help book so someone who isn't yourself can help you, that someone being the author. This is true of the whole self-help genre. It's true of how-to books, for example. And it's true of personal improvement books too. Some might even say it's true of religion books. But some others might say that those who say that should be pinned to the ground and bled dry with the slow slice of a blade across their throats. So it's wisest simply to note a divergence of views on that subcategory and move swiftly on.

None of the foregoing means self-help books are useless. On the contrary, they can be useful indeed. But it does mean that the idea of self in the land of self-help is a slippery one. And slippery can be good. Slippery can be pleasurable. Slippery can provide access to what would chafe if entered dry.

This book is a self-help book. Its objective, as it says on the cover, is to show you how to get filthy rich in rising Asia. And to do that it has to find you, huddled, shivering, on the packed earth under your mother's cot one cold, dewy morning. Your anguish is the anguish of a boy whose chocolate has been thrown away, whose remote controls are out of batteries, whose scooter is busted, whose new sneakers have been stolen. This is all the more remarkable since you've never in your life seen any of these things.

The whites of your eyes are yellow, a consequence of spiking bilirubin levels in your blood. The virus afflicting you is called hepatitis E. Its typical mode of transmission is fecal-oral. Yum. It kills only about one in fifty, so you're likely to recover. But right now you feel like you're going to die.

Your mother has encountered this condition many times, or conditions like it anyway. So maybe she doesn't think you're going to die. Then again, maybe she does. Maybe she fears it. Everyone is going to die, and when a mother like yours sees in a third-born child like you the pain that makes you whimper under her cot the way you do, maybe she feels your death push forward a few decades, take off its

dark, dusty headscarf, and settle with open-haired familiarity and a lascivious smile into this, the single mud-walled
room she shares with all of her surviving offspring.

What she says is, "Don't leave us here."

Your father has heard this request of hers before. This
does not make him completely unsusceptible to it, however.
He is a man of voracious sexual appetite, and he often thinks
while he is away of your mother's heavy breasts and solid,
ample thighs, and he still longs to thrust himself inside her
nightly rather than on just three or four visits per year. He
also enjoys her unusually rude sense of humor, and sometimes her companionship as well. And although he is not
given to displays of affection towards their young, he would
like to watch you and your siblings grow. His own father de-
rived considerable pleasure from the daily progress of crops
in the fields, and in this, at least insofar as it is analogous to
the development of children, the two men are similar.

He says, "I can't afford to bring you to the city."

"We could stay with you in the quarters."

"I share my room with the driver. He's a masturbating,
chain-smoking, flatulent sisterfucker. There are no families
in the quarters."

"You earn ten thousand now. You're not a poor man."

"In the city ten thousand makes you a poor man."

He gets up and walks outside. Your eyes follow him, his

leather sandals unslung at the rear, their straps flapping free, his chapped heels callused, hard, crustacean-like. He steps through the doorway into the open-air courtyard located at the center of your extended family's compound. He is unlikely to linger there in contemplation of the single, shade-giving tree, comforting in summer, but now, in spring, still tough and scraggly. Possibly he exits the compound and makes his way to the ridge behind which he prefers to defecate, squatting low and squeezing forcefully to expel the contents of his colon. Possibly he is alone, or possibly he is not.

Beside the ridge is a meaty gully as deep as a man is tall, and at the bottom of that gully is a slender trickle of water. In this season the two are incongruous, the skeletal inmate of a concentration camp dressed in the tunic of an obese pastry chef. Only briefly, during the monsoon, does the gully fill to anything near capacity, and that too is an occurrence less regular than in the past, dependent on increasingly fickle atmospheric currents.

The people of your village relieve themselves downstream of where they wash their clothes, a place in turn downstream of where they drink. Farther upstream, the village before yours does the same. Farther still, where the water emerges from the hills as a sometimes-gushing brook, it is partly employed in the industrial processes of an old, rusting, and subscale textile plant, and partly used as drainage for the fart-smelling gray effluent that results.

Your father is a cook, but despite being reasonably good at his job and originating in the countryside, he is not a man obsessed with the freshness or quality of his ingredients. Cooking for him is a craft of spice and oil. His food burns the tongue and clogs the arteries. When he looks around him here, he does not see prickly leaves and hairy little berries for an effervescent salad, tan stalks of wheat for a heavenly balloon of stone-ground, stove-top-baked flatbread. He sees instead units of backbreaking toil. He sees hours and days and weeks and years. He sees the labor by which a farmer exchanges his allocation of time in this world for an allocation of time in this world. Here, in the heady bouquet of nature's pantry, your father sniffs mortality.

Most of the men of the village who now work in the city do return for the wheat harvest. But it is still too early in the year for that. Your father is here on leave. Nonetheless he likely accompanies his brothers to spend his morning cutting grass and clover for fodder. He will squat, again, but this time sickle in hand, and his movements of gather-cut-release-waddle will be repeated over and over and over as the sun too retraces its own incremental path in the sky.

Beside him, a single dirt road passes through the fields. Should the landlord or his sons drive by in their SUV, your

father and his brothers will bring their hands to their fore-
heads, bend low, and avert their eyes. Meeting the gaze of a
landlord has been a risky business in these parts for centu-
ries, perhaps since the beginning of history. Recently some
men have begun to do it. But they have beards and earn
their keep in the seminaries. They walk tall, with chests
out. Your father is not one of them. In fact he dislikes them
almost as much as he does the landlords, and for the same
reasons. They strike him as domineering and lazy.

Lying on your side with one ear on the packed earth,
from your erect-worm's-height perspective you watch your
mother follow your father into the courtyard. She feeds the
water buffalo tethered there, tossing fodder cut yesterday
and mixed with straw into a wooden trough, and milks the
animal as it eats, jets of liquid smacking hard into her tin
pail. When she is done, the children of the compound, your
siblings and cousins, lead the buffalo, its calf, and the goats
out to forage. You hear the swishing of the peeled branches
they hold and then they are gone.

Your aunts next leave the compound, bearing clay pots
on their heads for water and carrying clothes and soap
for cleaning. These are social tasks. Your mother's responsibility is solitary. Her alone, them together. It is not
a coincidence. She squats as your father is likely squatting,
handle-less broom in her hand instead of a sickle, her sweep-

sweep-waddle approximating his own movements. Squatting is energy efficient, better for the back and hence ergonomic, and it is not painful. But done for hours and days and weeks and years its mild discomfort echoes in the mind like muffled screams from a subterranean torture chamber. It can be borne endlessly, provided it is never acknowledged.

Your mother cleans the courtyard under the gaze of her mother-in-law. The old woman sits in shadow, the edge of her shawl held in her mouth to conceal not her attributes of temptation but rather her lack of teeth, and looks on in unquenchable disapproval. Your mother is regarded in the compound as vain and arrogant and headstrong, and these accusations have bite, for they are all true. Your grandmother tells your mother she has missed a spot. Because she is toothless and holds the cloth between her lips, her words sound like she is spitting.

Your mother and grandmother play a waiting game. The older woman waits for the younger woman to age, the younger woman waits for the older woman to die. It is a game both will inevitably win. In the meantime, your grandmother flaunts her authority when she can, and your mother flaunts her physical strength. The other women of the compound would be frightened of your mother were it not for the reassuring existence of the men. In an all-female

society your mother would likely rise to be queen, a bloody
staff in her hand and crushed skulls beneath her feet. Here
the best she has been able to manage is for the most part to
be spared severe provocation. Even this, cut off as she is
from her own village, is no small victory.

Unsaid between your mother and your father is that on
ten thousand a month he could, just barely, afford to bring
your mother and you children to the city. It would be tight
but not impossible. At the moment he is able to send most of
his salary back to the village, where it is split between your
mother and the rest of the clan. If she and you children were
to move in with him, the flow of his money to this place
would slow to a trickle, swelling like the water in the gully
only in the two festival months when he could perhaps expect a bonus and hopefully would not have debts to clear.

You watch your mother slice up a lengthy white radish
and boil it over an open fire. The sun has banished the dew,
and even unwell as you are, you no longer feel cold. You feel
weak, though, and the pain in your gut is as if a parasite is
eating you alive from within. So you do not resist as your
mother lifts your head off the earth and ladles her elixir into
your mouth. It smells like a burp, like the gasses from a
man's belly. It makes your gorge rise. But you have nothing
inside that you can vomit, and you drink it without incident.

As you lie motionless afterwards, a young jaundiced village boy, radish juice dribbling from the corner of your lips and forming a small patch of mud on the ground, it must seem that getting filthy rich is beyond your reach. But have faith. You are not as powerless as you appear. Your moment is about to come. Yes, this book is going to offer you a choice.

Decision time arrives a few hours later. The sun has set and your mother has shifted you onto the cot, where you lie swaddled in a blanket even though the evening is warm. The men have returned from the fields, and the family, all except you, have eaten together in the courtyard. Through your doorway you can hear the gurgle of a water pipe and see the flare of its coals as one of your uncles inhales.

Your parents stand over you, looking down. Tomorrow your father will return to the city. He is thinking.

"Will you be all right?" he asks you.

It is the first question he has asked you on this visit, perhaps the first sentence he has uttered to you directly in months. You are in pain and frightened. So the answer is obviously no.

Yet you say, "Yes."

And take your destiny into your own hands.

Your father absorbs your croak and nods. He says to your mother, "He's a strong child. This one."

She says, "He's very strong."

You'll never know if it is your answer that makes your

father change his answer. But that night he tells your mother that he has decided she and you children will join him in the city.

They seal the deal with sex. Intercourse in the village is a private act only when it takes place in the fields. Indoors, no couple has a room to themselves. Your parents share theirs with all three of their surviving children. But it is dark, so little is visible. Moreover, your mother and father remain almost entirely clothed. They have never in their lives stripped naked to copulate.

Kneeling, your father loosens the drawstring of his baggy trousers. Lying with her stomach on the floor, your mother pivots her pelvis and does the same. She reaches behind to tug on him with her hand, a firm and direct gesture not unlike her milking of the water buffalo this morning, but she finds him already ready. She rises onto all fours. He enters her, propping himself up with one hand and using the other on her breast, alternately to fondle and for purchase as he pulls himself forward. They engage in a degree of sound suppression, but muscular grunting, fleshy impact, traumatized respiration, and hydraulic suction nonetheless remain audible. You and your siblings sleep or pretend to sleep until they are done. Then they join you on your mother's cot, exhausted, and are within moments lost in their dreams. Your mother snores.

A month later you are well enough to ride with your brother and sister on the roof of the overloaded bus that bears your family and threescore cramped others to the city. If it tips over as it careens down the road, swerving in mad competition with other equally crowded rivals as they seek to pick up the next and next groups of prospective passengers on this route, your likelihood of death or at least dismemberment will be extremely high. Such things happen often, although not nearly as often as they don't happen. But today is your lucky day.

Gripping ropes that mostly succeed in binding luggage to this vehicle, you witness a passage of time that outstrips its chronological equivalent. Just as when headed into the mountains a quick shift in altitude can vault one from subtropical jungle to semi-arctic tundra, so too can a few hours on a bus from rural remoteness to urban centrality appear to span millennia.

Atop your inky-smoke-spewing, starboard-listing conveyance you survey the changes with awe. Dirt streets give way to paved ones, potholes grow less frequent and soon all but disappear, and the kamikaze rush of oncoming traffic vanishes, to be replaced by the enforced peace of the dual carriageway. Electricity makes its appearance, first in passing as you slip below a steel parade of high-voltage giants, then later in the form of wires running at bus-top eye level on either side of the road, and finally in streetlights and shop signs and glorious, magnificent billboards. Buildings go from mud to brick to concrete, then shoot up to an unimaginable four stories, even five.

At each subsequent wonder you think you have arrived, that surely nothing could belong more to your destination than this, and each time you are proven wrong until you cease thinking and simply surrender to the layers of marvels and visions washing over you like the walls of rain that follow one another seemingly endlessly in the monsoon, endlessly that is until they end, without warning, and then the bus shudders to a stop and you are finally, irrevocably there.

As you and your parents and siblings dismount, you embody one of the great changes of your time. Where once your clan was innumerable, not infinite but of a large number not readily known, now there are five of you. Five. The fingers on one hand, the toes on one foot, a minuscule aggregation when compared with shoals of fish or flocks of birds or indeed tribes of humans. In the history of the evolution of the family, you and the millions of other migrants like you represent an ongoing proliferation of the nuclear. It is an explosive transformation, the supportive, stifling, stabilizing bonds of extended relationships weakening and giving way, leaving in their wake insecurity, anxiety, productivity, and potential.

Moving to the city is the first step to getting filthy rich in rising Asia. And you have now taken it. Congratulations. Your sister turns to look at you. Her left hand steadies the enormous bundle of clothing and possessions balanced on her head. Her right hand grips the handle of a cracked and battered suitcase likely discarded by its original owner around the time your father was born. She smiles and you smile in return, your faces small ovals of the familiar in an otherwise unrecognizable world. You think your sister is trying to reassure you. It does not occur to you, young as you are, that it is she who needs reassurance, that she seeks you out not to comfort you, but rather for the comfort that you, her only recently recovered little brother, have in this moment of fragile vulnerability the capacity to offer her.

TWO

GET AN EDUCATION

IT'S REMARKABLE HOW MANY BOOKS FALL INTO THE category of self-help. Why, for example, do you persist in reading that much-praised, breathtakingly boring foreign novel, slogging through page after page after please-make-it-stop page of tar-slow prose and blush-inducing formal conceit, if not out of an impulse to understand distant lands that because of globalization are increasingly affecting life in your own? What is this impulse of yours, at its core, if not a desire for self-help?

And what of the other novels, those which for reasons of plot or language or wisdom or frequent gratuitous and graphic sex you actually enjoy and read with delighted hunger? Surely those too are versions of self-help. At the very least they help you pass the time, and time is the stuff of which a self is made. The same goes for narrative nonfiction, and doubly so for non-narrative nonfiction.

Indeed, all books, each and every book ever written, could be said to be offered to the reader as a form of self-help. Textbooks, those whores, are particularly explicit in acknowledging this, and it is with a textbook that you, at this moment, after several years in the city, are walking down the street.

Your city is not laid out as a single-celled organism, with a wealthy nucleus surrounded by an ooze of slums. It lacks sufficient mass transit to move all of its workers twice daily in the fashion this would require. It also lacks, since the end of colonization generations ago, governance powerful enough to dispossess individuals of their property in sufficient numbers. Accordingly, the poor live near the rich. Wealthy neighborhoods are often divided by a single boulevard from factories and markets and graveyards, and those in turn may be separated from the homes of the impoverished only by an open sewer, railroad track, or narrow alley. Your own triangle-shaped community, not atypically, is bounded by all three.

Arriving at your destination, you see a whitewashed building with a plaque declaring its name and function. This is your school, and it is wedged between a tire-repair stall and a corner kiosk that derives the bulk of its revenues from the sale of cigarettes. Until the age of about twelve, when the opportunity cost of forgone wages becomes significant, most children in your area do in fact manage to go to school. Most, but by no means all. A boy your height is working shirtless in the tire-repair stall. He watches you now as you pass.

There are fifty pupils in your class and stools for thirty. The others sit on the floor or stand. You are instructed by a single hollow-cheeked, betel-nut-spitting, possibly tubercular teacher. Today he takes you through your multiplication tables. This he does in a distracted chant, his preferred, indeed only, pedagogical tool being enforced rote memorization. Parts of his mind not responsible for control over the tissue and bone of his vocal apparatus wander far, far away.

Your teacher chants, "Ten tens, a hundred."

The class chants it back.

Your teacher chants, "Eleven elevens, a hundred twenty-one."

The class chants it back.

Your teacher chants, "Twelve twelves, a hundred thirty-four."

One foolhardy voice interrupts. It says, "Forty-four."

There is a hushed silence. The voice is yours. You spoke without thinking, or at least without thinking sufficiently ahead.

Your teacher says, "What did you say?"

You hesitate. But it has happened. There is no way back.

"Forty-four."

Your teacher's tone is soft with menace. "Why did you say that?"

"Twelve twelves are a hundred forty-four."

"You think I'm an idiot?"

"No, sir. I thought you said a hundred thirty-four. I made a mistake. You said a hundred forty-four. I'm sorry, sir."

The entire class knows your teacher did not say a hundred forty-four. Or perhaps not the entire class. Much of the class was paying no attention, daydreaming of kites or assault rifles, or rolling nasal residue into balls between their thumbs and forefingers. But some of them know. And all of them know what will happen next, if not the precise form it will take. They watch now in horrified fascination, like seals on a rock observing a great white breaching beneath one of their own, just a short swim away.

Most of you have in the past been punished by your teacher. You, as one of the brightest students, have drawn some of the most severe punishments. You attempt to hide your knowledge, but every so often bravado gets the better of you and it comes out, as it just has, and then there is hell to pay. Today your teacher reaches into the pocket of his tunic, where he keeps a small amount of coarse sand, and grips you by the ear, the sand on his fingertips adding abrasion to the enormous pressure he applies, so that your earlobe is not only crushed but also made raw and slightly bloody. You refuse to cry out, denying your torturer satisfaction, and ensuring thereby that the punishment you receive is prolonged.

Your teacher did not want to be a teacher. He wanted to be a meter reader at the electric utility. Meter readers do not have to put up with children, work comparatively little, and what is more important, have greater opportunity for corruption and are hence both better off and held in higher regard by society. Nor was becoming a meter reader out of your teacher's reach. His uncle worked for the electric utility. But the one position as meter reader this uncle was able to facilitate went, as all things most desirable in life invariably went, to your teacher's elder brother.

So your teacher, who narrowly failed his secondary-school final examination but was able to have the results falsified, and with his false results, a bribe equivalent to sixty percent of one year's prospective salary, and a good low-level connection in the education bureaucracy in the form of a cousin, secured only the post he currently occupies. He is not exactly a man who lives to teach. In fact he hates to teach. It shames him. Nonetheless he retains a small but not nonexistent fear of losing his job, of somehow being found out, or if not losing his job then at least being put in a position where he will be forced to pay yet another and indeed larger bribe in order to retain it, and this fear, augmented by his sense of abiding disappointment and his not unfounded conviction that the world is profoundly unfair, manifests itself in the steady dose of violence he visits upon his charges. With each blow, he tells himself, he helps education penetrate another thick skull.

Penetration and education, the two are intertwined in the lives of many around you. In the life of your sister, for example. She is sobbing when you return home. Lately she alternates with alarming frequency between suppressed but globular tears and calm airs of smug superiority. At the moment it is the former.

You say, "Again?"

"Sit on my dick, you little pussy."

You shake your head. You are too weak to retort appropriately, and what's more too drained to be confident of dodging one of her quick-fire slaps.

She notices something is wrong with you. She says, "What happened to your ear?"

"Teacher."

"That sisterfucker. Come here."

You sit beside her and she puts her arm around you,

stroking your hair. You shut your eyes. She sniffles once or twice, but she is done crying for now.

You say, "Are you frightened?"

"Frightened?" She forces a laugh. "He should be frightened of me."

The he she refers to is your father's second cousin, a decade her senior, to whom she is now betrothed. His first wife recently died in childbirth after two earlier miscarriages, and no time has been wasted in arranging him another.

"Does he still have that mustache?" you ask.

"How should I know? I haven't seen him in years."

"It's enormous. That mustache."

"You know what they say about the size of a man's mustache."

"What?"

"Never mind."

"So are you frightened?"

"Of what?"

"I don't know. Of leaving. I'd be scared to move back to the village all by myself."

"That's why you're still a boy and I'm a woman."

"You're a girl."

"No, I'm a woman."

"A girl."

"I bleed every month. I'm a woman."

"You're disgusting."

"Maybe." She smiles. "But a woman."

Then she surprises you. She does something you associate with women of girth and substance, not with slender slips of girls like your sister. She sings. She sings in a quiet and powerful voice. She sings a song that mothers in your village sing to their newborns, a song that your mother in fact sang to each of you. It is like a lullaby but more upbeat, meant not to put an infant to sleep but rather to communicate a mother's presence when a task takes her beyond touch or out of sight. You have not heard it in years. It feels strange to hear your sister sing it, oddly relaxing and unsettling at the same time. You lean against her as she sings, and you feel her body swell and diminish like a harmonium.

When she stops, you say, "Let's play river."

"All right."

The two of you leave the room shared by your family, similar in size to the room you shared in your village, but made of brick instead of mud and perched precariously on the third and highest floor of a tottering, narrow building. You dash down the stairwell and from there find your way to a small, secluded alley, or inlet, rather, since it branches off the street but leads nowhere, and is circumscribed by dwellings on three sides. It contains a hillock of trash, behind which is an uncovered sewer.

Viewing the scene from the lenses of an orbiting reconnaissance satellite, an observer would see two children behaving peculiarly. He or she would note that they display undue caution in approaching the sewer, as if it were not a trickle of excrement of varying viscosities but rather a gushing torrent. Moreover, although the sewer is shallow and could be crossed with a modest hop, the children stand warily on either side of it, cupping their hands to their mouths as though shouting to each other from a great distance. Agreement reached, one picks up a piece of metal, the discarded spoke of a bicycle wheel, perhaps, and seems to use it to fish, albeit with no string or bait, and no prospect of catching anything. The other takes a torn strip of brown cardboard packaging, long and jagged, and jabs it repeatedly in the direction of the sewer. Spearing transparent turtles? Fending off invisible crocodiles? It is difficult to gauge the purpose of her frenetic movements. Suddenly the girl squats, pantomiming the gestures of lighting a fire. The boy calls out to her, and she tosses him one end of her shawl.

You grip the shawl firmly. In your hands it becomes the rope you will use to ford the river. But before you can do so, and without warning, the spell breaks. You follow your sister's altered gaze and see that a formerly shuttered window is now open. A tall, bald man stands inside, staring at your sister intently. She takes her shawl from you and throws one end over her head, the other across her still-small-breasted chest.

She says, "Let's go home."

Your sister has worked as a cleaning girl since shortly after your family moved to the city, your father's income unable to keep up with the rampant inflation of recent years. She was told she could go back to school once your brother, the middle of you three surviving siblings, was old enough to work. She demonstrated more enthusiasm for education in her few months in a classroom than your brother did in his several years. He has just been found employment as a painter's assistant, and has been taken out of school as a result, but your sister will not be sent there in his stead. Her time for that has passed. Marriage is her future. She has been marked for entry.

Your brother is sitting in the room when the two of you return. He is exhausted, a fine white dusting of paint on the exposed skin of his hands and face. It is also on his hair, like a play actor's makeup, and he resembles a boy about to go onstage as a middle-aged man in a school drama. He looks at you wearily and coughs.

Your sister says, "I told you, you shouldn't smoke."

He says, "I don't smoke."

She sniffs him. "Yes, you do."

"The master does. I'm just around him all day."

The truth is that your brother has smoked on several occasions. But he does not particularly like to smoke, and he has not smoked this week. Besides, smoking is not the reason for his cough. The reason for his cough is paint inhalation.

Each morning your brother walks over the train tracks, using the crossing if it is open, or if it is not and the train is moving slowly, making a dash for it with the urchins for whom this activity is a game. He catches a bus to the century-old, and hence in city historical terms neither recent nor ancient, European-designed commercial district. There he enters, through a tea stall, an open space that was formerly a public square, or public trapezoid rather, but is now, because of illegally built encroachments that have filled in its entryways, an entirely enclosed courtyard.

The courtyard is a marvel of mixed-use planning, or non-planning to be more precise. The upper floors of its constituent buildings contain family and labor residences, guest rooms of a run-down hotel, workshops occupied by tailors, embroiderers, and other craftsmen, and also offices, including two belonging to a pair of aging private investigators who harbor an abiding hatred and can be seen watching each other through their windows from either side of the divide. At ground level, the fronts of the buildings, which is to say their non-courtyard-facing sides, are given over to shops and unprepossessing restaurants. Their courtyard-facing backsides, on the other hand, are devoted to small-scale manufacturing, to operations that because of their sonic, aromatic, visual, or chemical noxiousness are unpopular in a high-density neighborhood such as this one, and therefore utilize the enclosed courtyard as a partial veil.

The painter your brother assists is an air-gun spray painter, and their work today was an assignment for an interior designer of remarkable valor and renown. Your brother began by unloading a set of custom-made, built-in bookshelves, still unpainted and yet to be built in, from a tiny flatbed truck. He carried them with great care, in small hop-like increments because of their weight, through the tea stall, out into the courtyard, and back into the entrance of the painter's shed. He taped plastic sheets to the corrugated ceiling, forming curtains to prevent paint particles from drifting onto the surfaces of other objects already painted and awaiting collection. He taped newspaper around the halogen lighting fixtures and the brushed-metal electricity switches that were built into the built-in bookshelves. He lifted cans to the painter's instructions, mixing paint and primer. He located extension cords to power up the compressor for the air gun. He then stood behind the painter, sweating in unventilated, infernally hot conditions, as the painter held the gun and proceeded to make hundreds of straight-line passes across the wood of the bookshelves, like a robot in an automotive assembly plant, but with slightly less precision and considerably more swearing, your brother dashing off every few minutes in response to grunted commands to clean a spill, move the ladder, get some water, get some bread, or reconnect exposed wires with electrical tape.

Your brother's work is in some senses like being an astronaut, or slightly more prosaically, a scuba diver. It too involves the hiss of air, the feeling of weightlessness, the sudden pressure headaches and nausea, the precariousness that results when an organic being and a machine are fused together. Then again, an astronaut or aquanaut sees unimaginable new worlds, whereas your brother sees only a monocolor haze of varying intensities.

His occupation requires patience and the fortitude to withstand a constant sense of low-level panic, both of which out of necessity your brother has acquired. In theory it also requires protection in the form of goggles and respirators, but these are clearly optional, as your brother and his master have neither, placing thin cotton rags over their mouths and noses instead. Hence, in the near term, your brother's cough. Over the long term, consequences can be more serious. But a painter's assistant is paid, the skills he learns are valuable, and in any case over sufficiently long a term, as everyone knows, there is nothing that does not have as its consequence death.

As your mother prepares dinner that evening, a lentil stew thickened with chunks of onion, not because onions are her favorite ingredient but because they appear to add substance to a meal and today in the market they were cheap, it may not seem that you are a lucky child. Your wounded ear is, after all, more visibly painful than the expression in your sister's eyes or the residue of paint on your brother's skin. Yet you are fortunate. Fortunate in being third-born.

Getting an education is a running leap towards becoming filthy rich in rising Asia. This is no secret. But like many desirable things, simply being well known does not make it easily achieved. There are forks in the road to wealth that have nothing to do with choice or desire or effort, forks that have to do with chance, and in your case, the order of your birth is one of these. Third means you are not heading back to the village. Third means you are not working as a painter's assistant. Third also means you are not, like the fourth of you three surviving siblings, a tiny skeleton in a small grave at the base of a tree.

Your father comes home after you have eaten. He has his meals with the other servants at the house where he cooks. All of you crowd around the family television, a sign of your urban prosperity. It is powered by a wire of communally stolen electricity that runs down the front of your building. It is archaic, a black-and-white, cathode-ray-tube device with an excessively curved and annoyingly chipped screen. It is narrower than the distance between your wrist and your elbow. And it is able to capture only the few channels that broadcast terrestrially. But it works, and your family watches in a state of hushed rapture the musical variety show it delivers to your room.

When the show is done, credits roll. Your mother sees a meaningless stream of hieroglyphs. Your father and sister make out an occasional number, your brother that and the occasional word. For you alone does this part of the programming make sense. You understand it reveals who is responsible for what.

The electricity to your neighborhood cuts out on the hour, and with it the light from your single naked bulb. A candle burns while you all prepare to turn in, and is then extinguished by your mother with a squeeze of her fingers.

In the room it is now dim but not dark, the glow of the city creeping in through your shutters, and quiet but not silent. You hear a train decelerate as it passes along the tracks. You tend to sleep deeply, so although you share a cot, your brother's cough does not disturb you even once during the night.

THREE

DON'T FALL IN LOVE

MANY SELF-HELP BOOKS OFFER ADVICE ON HOW TO fall in love or, more to the point, how to make the object of your desire fall in love with you. This, to be absolutely clear, is not one of those self-help books. Because as far as getting rich is concerned, love can be an impediment. Yes, the pursuit of love and the pursuit of wealth have much in common. Both have the potential to inspire, motivate, uplift, and kill. But whereas achieving a massive bank balance demonstrably attracts fine physical specimens desperate to give their love in exchange, achieving love tends to do the opposite. It dampens the fire in the steam furnace of ambition, robbing of essential propulsion an already fraught upriver journey to the heart of financial success.

So it is worrisome that you, in the late middle of your

teenage years, are infatuated with a pretty girl. Her looks would not traditionally have been considered beautiful. No milky complexion, raven tresses, bountiful bosom, or soft, moon-like face for her. Her skin is darker than average, her hair and eyes lighter, making all three features a strikingly similar shade of brown. This bestows upon her a smoky quality, as though she has been drawn with charcoal. She is also lean, tall, and flat-chested, her breasts the size, as your mother notes dismissively, of two cheap little squashed mangoes.

"A boy who wants to fuck a thing like that," your mother says, "just wants to fuck another boy."

Perhaps. But you are not the pretty girl's only admirer. In fact, legions of boys your age turn to watch her as she walks by, her jaunty strut sticking out in your neighborhood like a bikini in a seminary. Maybe it's a generational thing. You boys, unlike your fathers, have grown up in the city, bombarded by imagery from television and billboards. Excessive fertility is here a liability, not an asset as historically it has been in the countryside, where food was for the most part grown rather than bought, and work could be found even for unskilled pairs of hands, though now there too that time is coming to an end.

Whatever the reason, the pretty girl is the object of much desire, anguish, and masturbatory activity. And she seems for her part to have some mild degree of interest in you. You have always been a sturdy fellow, but you are currently impressively fit. This is partly the consequence of a daily regimen of decline feet-on-cot push-ups, hang-from-stair pull-ups, and weighted brick-in-hand crunches and back extensions taught to you by the former competitive bodybuilder, now middle-aged gunman, who lives next door. And it is partly the consequence of your night job as a DVD delivery boy.

Beyond your neighborhood is a strip of factories, and beyond that is a market at the edge of a more prosperous bit of town. The market is built on a roundabout, and among its shops is a video retailer, dark and dimly lit, barely large enough to accommodate three customers at the same time, with two walls entirely covered in movie posters and a third obscured by a single, moderately packed shelf of DVDs. All sell for the same low price, a mere twofold markup on the retail price of a blank DVD. It goes without saying that they are pirated.

Because of splintering consumer tastes, the proprietor keeps only a hundred or so best-selling titles in stock at any given time. But, recognizing the substantial combined demand for films that each sell just one or two copies a year, he has established in his back room a dedicated high-speed broadband connection, disc-burning equipment, and

a photo-quality color printer. Customers can ask for virtually any film and he will have it dropped off to them the
same day.

Which is where you come in. The proprietor has divided
his delivery area into two zones. For the first zone, reach-
able on bicycle within a maximum of fifteen minutes, he has
his junior delivery boy, you. For the second zone, parts of
the city beyond that, he has his senior delivery boy, a man
who zooms through town on his motorcycle. This man's
salary is twice yours, and his tips several times greater, for
although your work is more strenuous, a man on a motorcycle is immediately perceived as a higher-end proposition
than a boy on a bicycle. Unfair, possibly, but you at least
do not have to pay monthly installments to a viciously
scarred and dangerously unforgiving moneylender for your
conveyance.

Your shift is six hours long, in the evening from seven to
one, its brief periods of intense activity interspersed with
lengthy lulls, and because of this you have developed speed
as well as stamina. You have also been exposed to a wide
range of people, including to women, who in the homes of
the rich think nothing of meeting you alone at the door,
alone, that is, if you do not count their watchful guards and
drivers and other outdoor servants, and then asking you
questions, often about image and sound quality but also

sometimes about whether a movie is good or not. As a result you know the names of actors and directors from all over the world, and what film should be compared with what, even in the cases of actors and directors and films you have not yourself seen, there being only so much off-time during your shifts to watch what happens to be playing at the shop.

In the same market works the pretty girl. Her father, a notorious drunk and gambler rarely sighted during the day, sends out his wife and daughter to earn back what he has lost the night before or will lose the night to come. The pretty girl is an assistant in a beauty salon, where she carries towels, handles chemicals, brings tea, sweeps hair off the floor, and massages the heads, backs, buttocks, thighs, and feet of women of all ages who are either wealthy or wish to appear wealthy. She also provides soft drinks to men waiting in cars for their wives and mistresses.

Her shift ends around the time yours begins, and since you live on adjacent streets you frequently pass each other on your ways to and from work. Sometimes you don't, and then you walk your bicycle by the salon to catch a glimpse of her inside. For her part, she seems fascinated by the video shop, and stares with particular interest at the ever-changing posters and DVD covers. She does not stare at you, but when your eyes meet, she does not look away.

Every so often it happens that you don't pass her on your

way to work and also don't see her when you walk by the windows of the salon. On these occasions you wonder where she might have gone. Perhaps she has a rotating day off in addition to the day the salon shuts. Such arrangements are, after all, not unheard of.

One winter evening, when it is already dark, and the two of you approach each other in the unlit alley that cuts through the factories, she speaks to you.

"You know a lot about movies?" she asks.

You get off your bicycle. "I know everything about movies."

She doesn't slow down. "Can you get me the best one? The one that's most popular?"

"Sure." You turn to keep pace with her. "You have a player to watch it on?"

"I will. Stop following me."

You halt as though at the lip of a precipice.

That night a video is quietly stolen from your shop. You carry it under your tunic the following day, but there is no sign of the pretty girl, neither on the way to work nor in her salon. You next see her the day after, her shawl halfheartedly draped over her head in a disdainful nod to the accepted norms of your neighborhood, as it always is when she is out on the street. She walks awkwardly, burdened with a large plastic bag containing a carton for a combination television and DVD player.

"Where did you get that?" you ask.

"A gift. My movie?"

"Here."

"Drop it in the bag."

You do. "That looks heavy. Can I help?"

"No. Anyway you're like me. Skinny."

"I'm strong."

"I didn't say we weren't strong."

She continues on her way, adding nothing further, not even a thank-you. You spend the rest of the evening in turmoil. Yes, you have spoken to the pretty girl twice. But she has given you no sign that she intends to speak to you again. Moreover, the strong-versus-skinny debate has been raging in your head for some time, so her comments cut close to the bone.

When asked why, despite your regular workouts, your physique looks nothing like his in photos of him at his competitive prime, your neighbor, the bodybuilder turned gunman, blames your diet. You are not getting enough protein.

"You're also young," he says, leaning against his doorway and taking a hit of his joint while a little girl clings to his leg. "You won't be at your max for another few years. But don't worry about it. You're tough. Not just here." He taps your bicep, which you flex surreptitiously beneath your tunic. "But here." He taps you between the eyes. "That's why the other kids usually don't mess with you."

"Not because they know I know you?"

He winks. "That too."

It's true that you have earned a savage reputation in the street brawls that break out among the boys of your neighborhood. But the issue of protein is one that rankles. These are relatively good times for your family. With one less mouth to feed since your sister returned to the village, and three earners since you joined your father and brother in employment, your household's per capita income is at an all-time high.

Still, protein is prohibitively expensive. Chicken is served in your home on the rarest of occasions, and red meat is a luxury to be enjoyed solely at grand celebrations, such as weddings, for which hosts save for many years. Lentils and spinach are of course staples of your diet, but vegetable protein is not the same thing as the animal stuff. After debt payments and donations to needy extended relatives, your immediate family is only able to afford a dozen eggs per week, or four each for your mother, brother, and you, and a half-liter of milk per day, of which your share works out to half a glass.

For the past several months, your one secret indulgence, which you are both deeply guilty about and fiercely committed to, has been the daily purchase of a quarter-liter packet of milk. This consumes ten percent of your salary, the precise amount of a raise you neglected to inform your father you received. Per week, your milk habit is also roughly equivalent to the price your employer's customers are willing to pay for the delivery of one pirated DVD, a fact that alternately angers you in its preposterousness and soothes you by putting your theft from your family into diminished perspective. The daily sum of money involved is, after all, worth a mere thumb's-width slice of a disc of plastic.

You are thinking of your complicated protein situation when you spy the pretty girl the next evening. This time she stops in the alley, produces the DVD you gave her, and thumps it without a word against your chest.

"You didn't like it?"

"I liked it."

"You can keep it. It's a gift."

Her face hardens. "I don't want gifts from you."

"I'm sorry."

"Do you have a phone?"

"Yes."

"Give it to me."

"Well, the problem is it's from work . . ."

She laughs. It is the first time you have seen her do so. It makes her look young. Or rather, since she is in fact young and normally appears more mature than her years, it makes her look her age.

She says, "Don't worry. I'm not going to take it with me."

You hand over your phone. She presses the keys and a single note emerges from her bag before she hangs up.

She says, "Now I have your number."

"And I have yours." You try to match her cool tone. It is unclear to you if you succeed, but in any case she is already walking away.

Because of the nature of your work and the need to be able to reach you on your delivery rounds at any moment, your employer has provided you with a mobile. It is a flimsy, thirdhand device, but a source of considerable pride nonetheless. Paying for outbound calls is your own responsibility, so you maintain a bare minimum of credit in your account. Tonight, though, you rush to buy a sizable refill card in anticipation.

But the call you are waiting for does not come. And when you try calling the pretty girl, she does not answer.

Deflated, you go about the rest of your deliveries without enthusiasm. Only at the end of your shift, after midnight, does she ring.

"Hi," she says.

"Hi."

"I want another movie."

"Which one?"

"I don't know. Tell me about the one I just saw."

"You want to see it again?"

She laughs. Twice in one night. You are pleased.

"No, you idiot. I want to know more about it."

"Like what?"

"Like everything. Who's in it? What else have they done? What do people talk about when they talk about it? Why is it popular?"

So you tell her. At first you stick to what you know, and when that runs out, and she asks for more, you say what you imagine could be plausible, and when she asks for even more, you venture into outright invention until she tells you she has heard enough.

"So how much of that was true?" she asks.

"Less than half. But definitely some."

She laughs again. "An honest boy."

"Where are your parents?"

"Why?"

"Just that they let you speak on the phone at this time."

"My father's out. And my mother's asleep."

"She doesn't wake up when you talk?"

"I'm on the roof."

You consider this. The image of her alone on a rooftop makes you somewhat breathless. But before you can think of anything appropriate to say, she speaks again.

"I'll take another tomorrow. You pick. But a popular one."

Thus begins a ritual that will last for several months. You meet on the way to work. Without stopping or exchanging a word, you either hand her a DVD or receive one she has just seen. At night you speak. Initially you feel like a professor of a subject in which you are barely literate, but because you give her only movies you have already partly seen, you are at least able to offer opinions of your own. Soon you find that she is helpfully filling in gaps in plot for you, telling you entire story lines, in fact. And your debates grow richer, and sometimes more heated. Your phone charges ought to be considerable, eating up most if not all of your tips, but she insists on being the one to call you, and so you spend nothing. She also insists the two of you do not discuss yourselves or your families.

The pretty girl's father is a trained stenographer who has not taken dictation, or held any other kind of employment, for some time. He always had weaknesses for cards and moonshine, but a lack of funds ensured in his case that these remained minor vices. His undoing came when his employer, the owner of a small plastic-bottle-manufacturing business, sold the company and rewarded the workers with bonuses. The pretty girl's father, having been in close daily contact with his departing boss, was treated with particular generosity, receiving over a year of his modest salary in a single lump sum. He never worked again.

A day in the life of the pretty girl's father now begins by going to sleep, which he does at dawn, rising at dusk or even later. He seizes what money he can from his wife and daughter and heads out to the bar, an underground establishment run by illegal African immigrants in a room that moves around the neighborhood, relocating each time the police, despite the bribes they receive, feel enough pressure from religious activists to make a show of shutting it down. He drinks alone until about midnight, when the game begins. Then he makes his way to the shuttered stall where his friends deal him in. Some of them have beaten him brutally in the past, one of the consequences of this being that he cannot bend three fingers on his left hand. He currently owes a substantial sum to a local gangster, an unsmiling man who is decidedly not his friend, and he plays in the hope of winning back this amount, and in the fear of what will happen if he does not.

His wife, the pretty girl's mother, suffers from severe and premature arthritis, a condition that makes her work as a sweepress, the only work she could find when circumstance thrust her relatively late in life into the paid labor force, an exercise in unmitigated agony. She no longer speaks to her husband, rarely speaks to the pretty girl except in occasional shrieks that can be heard up and down their street, and at her job pretends to be mute. She does speak to the divine, requesting to be released from her pain, and since she does so in public, mumbling seemingly to herself as she shuffles along, she is thought to be insane.

The pretty girl, not surprisingly, is planning her escape from her family. Her salary at the beauty salon is far more than what her mother makes, and she surrenders all of it to her parents without resistance. But the salon also caters to the needs of a number of lesser-known fashion photographers, so she has been exposed to their world, and has even been taken along to assist with hair and makeup on a few low-budget shoots. Through this she has become the mistress of a marketing manager responsible for a line of shampoo. He says he recognizes her potential to be a model, promises to make this happen, and in the meantime gives her gifts and cash. This cash the pretty girl has been saving, without telling either her parents or the marketing manager, believing that it represents her independence.

In exchange, the marketing manager demands physical favors. Initially these were kisses and permission to fondle her body. Then oral sex was required. This was followed by anal sex, which she believed, much to his surprise and delight, would allow her to preserve her virginity. But as the months passed, she came to doubt this logic, and eventually she permitted vaginal sex as well.

Whatever excitement and warmth the marketing manager once evoked in the pretty girl are now long gone. Her goal is sufficient funds to afford the rent of a place of her own, a goal she is now close to achieving. She also holds out some hope that the marketing manager will come through on his commitments to put her face in an ad and to introduce her to others who could further her career. But she is no fool, and she has been getting to know some of the photographers who use the services of her salon, more than one of whom has told her in no uncertain terms that she has potential.

What is clear to the pretty girl is that she must bridge a significant cultural and class divide to enter even the lower realms of the world of fashion. Hence her initial interest in movies, and in you. But she has discovered, beyond their educational value, that she actually enjoys films, and even more surprisingly, that she actually enjoys talking to you. In you she has made a friend, a person who renders her life in the neighborhood she hates more bearable.

She recognizes your feelings for her, however. She sees the way you look at her as you pass each other in the alley. Her own feelings for you, she tells herself, are rather different. She thinks of you with warmth and fondness, like a little brother, except of course that you are the same age, and not her brother at all. And you do have beautiful eyes.

Yes, she knows there is something. She is happy during her conversations with you, happier than at other times. She appreciates the lines of your body and how you carry yourself. She is amused by your manner. She is touched by your evident commitment. You are a door to an existence she does not desire, but even if the room beyond is repugnant, that door has won a portion of her affection.

So before she leaves the neighborhood for good, she gives you a call. This is itself not at all unusual. What she says, though, is.

"Come over."

"Where?"

"Meet me on my roof."

"Now?"

"Now."

"Where is it?"

"You know where it is."

You do not bother denying it. You have walked by her house many, many times. Every boy in your neighborhood knows where she lives. Though you have an hour left in your shift, you jump on your bicycle and pedal hard.

You climb the outside of her building carefully, moving

from wall to windowsill to ledge, trying not to be seen. When you get to the top she does not speak, and you, out of habit from your many unspeaking encounters, remain silent as well. She undresses you and lays you flat on the roof, and then she undresses herself. You see her navel, her ribs, her breasts, her clavicles. You watch her expose her body, taking in the shock of her nudity. A thigh flexes as she kneels. A brush strokes your belly. She mounts you, and you lie still, your arms stiff at your sides. She rides you slowly. Above her you see the lights of circling aircraft, a pair of stars able to burn through the city's pollution, lines of electrical wires dark against the glow of the night sky. She stares into your face and you look back until the pressure builds so strong that you have to look away. She pulls off before you ejaculate and finishes you with her hand.

After she has dressed, she says with a small smile, "I'm leaving."

She disappears downstairs. You have not kissed her. You have not even spoken.

The next day she is gone. You know it well before you fail to cross her on your way to work, word spreading quickly in your neighborhood that she has surrendered her honor and run away with her deflowerer. You are distraught. You are the sort of man who discovers love through his penis. You think the first woman you make love to should also be the last. Fortunately for you, for your financial prospects, she thinks of her second man as the one between her first and her third.

There are times when the currents leading to wealth can manage to pull you along regardless of whether you kick and paddle in the opposite direction.

Over dinner one night your mother calls the pretty girl a slut. You are so angry that you leave the room without finishing your egg, not hearing that in your mother's otherwise excoriating tone is a hint of wistfulness, and perhaps even of admiration.

FOUR

AVOID IDEALISTS

SURELY IDEALS, TRANSCENDING AS THEY DO PUNY humans and repositing meaning in vast abstract concepts instead, are by their very nature anti-self? It follows therefore that any self-help book advocating allegiance to an ideal is likely to be a sham. Yes, such self-help books are numerous, and yes, it's possible some of them do help a self, but more often than not, the self they help is their writer's self, not yours. So you'd do well to stay away, particularly if getting filthy rich tops your list of priorities.

What's true of self-help books is equally, and inevitably, true of people. Just as self-help books spouting idealism are best avoided, people so doing should be given wide berths too. These idealists tend to congregate around universities.

There they find an amenable environment of young, impressionable, malcontented, and ambitious individuals, individuals who, were they legends of yore instead of still-pimply and poor-personal-hygiene-sporting men and women in contemporary Asia, would be dashing off to slay dragons and triumph over genies, individuals, in other words, who give corporeal form to the term sucker.

You have, as was perhaps to be expected, fallen in with university idealists yourself. You sit at this moment on a narrow, lumpy bed in a hostel entirely appropriated by members of your organization, like a city block by a gang. Your hostel leader packs as you speak. He is a big man, tall as well as broad, with luxurious facial hair gone prematurely gray and the flattened features of a boxer.

"Where?" he asks you.

"Behind the space sciences building."

"How many of them?"

"Four. First years, I think."

"And you're sure it was hash?"

"I'm sure."

"We'll deal with it when I get back."

Sweat drips from you both. The electricity is out, and deprived of a fan the normally stifling room bakes in the heat like a charcoal-fired clay oven. Mosquitoes are rampant, having entered through the unrepaired mesh that now only partially covers the windows. You slap one feasting on your forearm as the hostel leader puts a pistol in his duffel bag and zips it shut.

Your father was adamant that you complete secondary school, even though you struggled to wake in the mornings after nights spent delivering DVDs. He recognized that in the city manliness is caught up in education. Burly though he is, your father had spent a working lifetime in the service of employers who, were the world a festival of unarmed banditry, he would have beaten, bound, and relieved of their possessions in a few quick minutes. He understood that his employers benefited from two things he lacked, advanced schooling and rampant nepotism. Unable to give his children the latter, he did all he could to ensure that at least one of you acquired the former.

Yet university is no easy proposition for a young man from a background such as yours. Nepotism is not restricted to swaggering about in its crudest, give-my-son-what-he-wants form. It frequently assumes more cunning guises, attire, for example, or an accent. Despite your previous academic results, and your familiarity with a wide range of personal styles and affectations from film, there was no hiding from the fact that you were the son of a servant. No soiree invitations awaited you, no rides in shiny new cars. Not even a cigarette shared among a half-dozen old friends on the university steps, for none from your school gained entry here save you.

State-subsidized though it may be, your university is exquisitely attuned to money. A small payment and exam invigilators are willing to overlook neighborly cheating. More and someone else can be sat in your seat to write your paper. More still and no writing is needed, blank exam books becoming, miraculously, a first-class result.

So you have grown a beard and joined an organization. As you speed away from the meeting with your hostel leader, other students avoid your gaze. No curious glances greet the sight of you and your bicycle, unusual on a campus where almost everyone without personal motorized transport travels by bus. The heat of the city, and its sprawl, have conspired to throw pedal power into disfavor among university types. But you are accustomed to it from your former job, and you value the exercise.

Compared with most of your comrades, you are more serious about your studies. You are also more sturdy and less easily frightened, and therefore better than most in a scrap. Many of your organization's leaders are in their late thirties, having ostensibly been students at the university for almost as long as you have been alive. In that respect, it is not your intention to follow in their footsteps. But you do relish the nervousness the sight of you now instills in wealthier pupils and corrupt administrators.

Your organization is, like all organizations, an economic enterprise. The product it sells is power. Some thirty thousand students attend your university. When combined with those at other institutions around the city, the street-filling capability of these young people becomes formidable, a show of force in the face of which unwanted laws, policies, and speech must tremble. Political parties seek to harness this with on-campus offshoots, of which yours is one.

In exchange for membership, you are given a monthly cash stipend, food and clothing, and a bed at the hostel. You are also given protection. Not only from other students, but from university officials, outsiders, and even the police. Pedaling down the streets of the city now, you know that you are not an isolated and impoverished individual, weak prey for the societally strong, punishable with a slap for being involved through no fault of your own in an accident between your bicycle and a car. No, you are part of something larger, something righteous. Something that is, if called upon to be, utterly ferocious.

As you ride you see the pretty girl on a billboard. She is modeling jeans. She poses as one of three young people, two female and one male, the others leaning their backs against each other and presenting their sides to the viewer, and so giving the impression to you of being a couple, while the pretty girl walks alone, perhaps signifying that she is single. This giant image creates conflicting emotions in you. You are struck, as always, by her beauty, and you are glad to be able to see her. You have heard through neighborhood rumor that she has split from the man she ran away with, and this composition, which creates the sense that she is available, is pleasing to you. But you also feel a stab of loss. The mobile number you had for her was immediately disconnected upon her departure, and you have not spoken to her, or seen her in person, since.

The pretty girl has finally succeeded in securing a place of her own, a room in an apartment she shares with a singer and an actress, both women in circumstances not dissimilar to hers. The marketing manager has been left behind, and she is now in an on-and-off relationship with a photographer, a long-haired fellow with an expensive motorcycle, who is thought by some to be bisexual. The pretty girl makes a modest living off print and runway work, having yet to establish what is known in her business as a name. At this very instant, recently awoken, and after skipping her lunch, she stands up in her lounge and takes a drag on a menthol cigarette, gazing out her window at scattered clouds bloodied by dust.

Beneath those clouds you dismount. You have been summoned to your home by your father because your mother is unwell. Your sister is again pregnant, so she cannot be here, but your brother and his wife have come. The unsightly bulge at your mother's throat upsets and shames her.

"If it weren't for my tits," she says, "everybody would think I'm a frog."

Despite her condition, the forcefulness in her eyes is undiminished. Unfortunately, much time has been wasted. Her normally robust health predisposed your mother to ignoring her symptoms. A neighborhood peddler of powdered herbs then fed her his concoctions for months, to no positive effect. The so-called doctor thereafter retained began a course of treatment that was halted only when it was discovered by you, chancing one day to watch him actually administering it, to consist entirely of saline injections and analgesic pills.

Your father has supplicated the matriarch of the family that currently employs him, a formerly tight-fisted widow who after her husband's passing has begun to engage in a measure of philanthropy, and she has agreed to intervene by arranging a trip to a private hospital.

The matriarch arrives outside your home in her car. She does not step out or open her door. She does not roll down her window. Your mother and sister-in-law are borne beside her on the rear seat, your father in front with the driver. You and your brother travel separately by bus, rejoining them in a hospital waiting room.

"Why are they here?" the old lady asks your father.

"These are my sons."

This seems to have little impact.

Your father adds, "This one's at university. He'll understand what the doctor says."

The old lady scrutinizes you, taking in your beard, your attire. She addresses your father again, "Only one of you will come inside."

"Him," your father says, indicating you.

The doctor is a plump, serious woman your mother's age. Her diagnosis upon examination, confirmed by test results at your second visit a week later, is papillary thyroid cancer. She explains that it is eminently treatable if dealt with early and appropriately. In your mother's case the opportunity to treat it early is long past, but surgical removal of the thyroid still carries hope.

"How much will this cost?" the matriarch asks.

"Including medicines, anesthesia, and recovery?"

"In a communal ward."

The doctor specifies a figure greater than your father's annual salary.

"And without the surgery?" the matriarch asks.

"She'll die."

The matriarch considers. You watch your mother. She stares fixedly ahead.

"Very well," the matriarch says.

The doctor silences a ringing mobile in the pocket of her smock. "Then there's ongoing treatment. Hormones, radiotherapy."

"That will be her family's responsibility. Is it likely the surgery alone will cure her?"

"It's possible."

"Good."

"But this is an advanced case. We'd normally expect to administer radioiodine a few weeks later, then . . ."

"Please explain all that to her family."

The doctor comes outside and does so. Your father looks at you repeatedly, and each time you nod. He is tearfully grateful to the matriarch for agreeing to pay for the surgery. He smiles and blinks and shifts his weight. He bows at the neck to her, again and again, a gesture like a nervous tic. You have not seen him in the presence of one of his employers since you were a child. To observe him like this disturbs you.

But you are struck most by your mother's expression. She has until now utterly refused to believe that she will not soon return to health.

"It won't be painful," you whisper to her. "They'll put you to sleep."

"I've pushed four of you out between my legs," she whispers back. "I can handle pain."

You smile, but only briefly, because looking at her you realize she is certain for the first time that her ailment will kill her.

Relations between your father and you have been tense, disapproving as he does of your beard and the organization you have joined. But over the following days he comes to lean on you heavily. There is deference in the way he watches you listen to a nurse or speak to a pharmacist or fill out a hospital form. He has never been a talkative man, but when you were younger he could be expressive physically, and he reverts to that mode of communication. He puts his arm around you. He pats your back. He ruffles your hair. These gestures feel good, even though it is strange that the man performing them has become shorter than you.

Your mother is taken home from her surgery alive. She is perplexed by her wounded status, like a soldier who has been shot but as yet sees no blood. The trauma her body sustained in the operating theater leaves her weak, and because the extraction of her thyroid and her lymph nodes involved the disassembly of considerable portions of her neck, she finds it difficult to speak. She is thus doubly disarmed, of her physical vitality and of her powerful tongue, and when not exhausted she is baffled, and at times angry.

Your family insists on maintaining that all will be well, with or without radiotherapy. You pretend to agree, but you also decide to approach your hostel leader for funds. He has just returned, his whereabouts while away a secret, and you find him in his room, reclining in torn socks upon his sweat-stained mattress.

"I need money," you say.

"That's a funny greeting, little brother."

"I'm sorry. My mother's sick."

"How much do you need?"

You name the figure.

"I see." He strokes his jaw slowly.

"I know it's a lot ..."

"It is a lot. But I think we can help you."

"Thank you."

"You should take her to one of our clinics."

"Our clinics?"

"Yes." He watches you. He has what should be a benevolent smile but his face remains impassive. You have seen him smile this way after breaking a man's nose.

"She's been treated at a private hospital. It's very good."

"Our clinics are very good. What's her illness?"

"Cancer."

"I'll make a few calls. Find out where she should go. Tell them to expect you."

You know better than to argue.

In the evenings you ride your bicycle to your home, staying with your parents until it is time for them to attempt to sleep. You do not wish to burden them with the costs of your meals, so you continue to board at the hostel, and besides, your membership of the organization is an occupation for which you are paid, if modestly, and on which your performance is assessed. Now in particular it is important that you be seen to be doing your job well. You attend meetings, read the organization's literature, and keep your eyes and ears open, as you have been instructed to do. But your thoughts wing their way to your mother.

Later that week you have the good fortune of again catching a group of students furtively smoking hash in a shed behind the space sciences building. You inform your leader, who tells you to accompany him to the scene. As you walk he looks around pleasantly at the plum-headed green parrots chattering in the treetops. You suspect he is carrying his gun.

He greets the smokers. There are five of them and two of you, but they appear very frightened.

"This is not good, my brothers," your leader says.

"What, sir?" one of them asks. He is a lanky fellow with

sideburns and a soul patch, his T-shirt suggesting an affinity for heavy metal.

Your leader cuffs him across the face and continues without raising his voice, "These drugs are forbidden. They will make you weak. You're intelligent boys. You should know that."

All five nod vigorously.

Your leader spreads his arms. "This won't happen again?"

He is assured that it will not.

The following day your leader gives you the details of a clinic. It is just outside the city, or at least outside what is currently thought of as the city, even though roadside urbanization links its location to the metropolis like the arm of an octopus. You and your mother journey there by bus. The clinic is a low building, almost equal in footprint but not in height to the place of worship that sits beside it. Its clientele is poor, and it utterly lacks the computers and air-conditioning, or for that matter the clean walls and floors, of the private hospital.

The doctor you are taken to see examines your mother quickly, looks at her test results, and shakes his head. "We can't help her," he says to you.

"You don't treat cancer?"

"Sometimes. Surgically. But we don't administer hormones or radiotherapy."

"What should we do?"

"You should pray. It's out of your hands. The thyroid has been removed. She might be fine."

Your mother is quiet throughout, as she tends to be in her interactions with medical professionals. They are unusual in their capacity to cause this behavior in her. Their power to kill in the future by uttering mysterious words today robs her of her confidence and she, a customarily confident woman, resents this. She longs to resist them but has no idea how to do so.

For a time, your mother's condition seems neither particularly good nor bad. The wound of the surgery heals, darkening and puckering under its protective dressing of gauze. She endures headaches stoically, refusing for the most part to admit to them but unable entirely to mask in her eyes signs of the discomfort they cause. She also has muscular twitches, little spasms thrusting beneath her shawl like fish feeding below the surface of a pond. You recognize these from your online investigations at the university computer center as being symptoms of her thyroid hormone deficiency.

Eventually your father beseeches his employer for further assistance. But the matriarch explains to him that life is one long series of illnesses, that she has intervened to save his wife, successfully and at great expense, but cannot be asked to keep intervening, again and again, for where would it stop, she is not made of money, and in the end, as she knows only too well herself, certain things are up to fate, and we can struggle, but fate is fate, so it would be best for him and his family to do what they can, since it is after all their responsibility, and to accept that she has already helped them more than anyone could reasonably have expected that she would.

In the coming months your mother's suffering is extreme, her cancer having metastasized to her bones and lungs. This is accompanied by a transformation in her appearance and personality. She is gripped by fear, surprised both by her unyielding attachment to life and by the failure of her imagination to conceive of a proud ending to it. Her death, in the absence of modern palliative care, is preceded by agony, only partially mitigated in her final fortnight by street heroin procured by your brother and administered by your father through slender, long-filtered women's cigarettes, from which your mother, wheezing, attempts to inhale in tiny gasps.

Your sister arrives from the village to comfort her. Neither woman has previously thought of your sister as your mother's favorite, that honor being yours, but it is to your sister that your mother turns most naturally at this time, perhaps because she is her eldest, or because they are both

women, or because your sister is the only one of her children to herself be a mother, and in your sister your mother
perceives echoes of her own mother, whom she last saw the
same age your sister is now, when your mother was a little
girl. In the moment she ceases to live, your sister is holding
your mother's hands, your mother like an infant struggling
to take its first breath as it transitions from aquatic life to
terrestrial, but in reverse, with her lungs filling with water,
and the breath never coming.

As you and the men of your family carry her white-
shrouded body on your shoulders to the open, dusty pit of
her grave, you are struck by how light she is. The speed
of her progression from solid heartiness to ephemeral fra-
gility has been so strange as to be almost fantastic. Rose
petals are thrown, incense lit, entreaties to the divine offered, and then those of you still living return to your lives.

At the university, members of your organization urge
you not to mourn too much or for more than the prescribed
period. They say that to do otherwise is to reject what fate
has decreed. Instead they tell you to focus your energies on
the tasks you are assigned, to recognize your comrades as
your true family, and to act through the organization to ful-
fill your destiny as your mother has fulfilled hers. But these
suggestions strike you as scripted and uncompelling, and
moreover in your current introspective and melancholy

state your appetite for the food, clothing, and belonging that the organization offers, and for the protection that it claims to offer, is significantly diminished.

Your leader begins to watch you, then tells those he trusts most among your comrades to watch you as well. He is troubled by your apathy and listlessness, by the note of cynicism you inject into conversations and meetings. You are careful never knowingly to provoke him, but he is aware of the negative influence you have begun to assert when you think him out of earshot. It does not take him long to gather evidence sufficient to issue you with a stern and possibly, given his volatility, painful reprimand, but when he dispatches his deputy to bring you to him, you are nowhere to be found.

Your father has taken your mother's passing hard, but has refused to accompany your sister back to the village or to stay for a time with your brother. He instead continues with his job, traveling to the matriarch's residence in the mornings and returning home at night. It is not your intention, when you move in with him, to stay permanently, yet as the days go by you show no interest in resuming your studies, and after a while you begin to hunt for a job.

One afternoon, as you ride your bicycle in pursuit of employment, you glimpse what you think is a familiar face in a small battered car stopped at a red light. You look closely and are certain that yes, it is the pretty girl. She rides in the driver's seat, alone, her face covered with thick makeup from a shoot. You smile and wave, but she does not see you, or if she does, then she does not recognize you, and when the light changes she careens off on her way.

It is perhaps not that night, but certainly that week, that you sit yourself down at a neighborhood roadside stall and ask a wrinkled old man with hennaed hair and a cutthroat razor finally to give you a shave.

FIVE

LEARN FROM
A MASTER

TO BE EFFECTIVE, A SELF-HELP BOOK REQUIRES TWO things. First, the help it suggests should be helpful. Obviously. And second, without which the first is impossible, the self it's trying to help should have some idea of what help is needed. For our collaboration to work, in other words, you must know yourself well enough to understand what you want and where you want to go. Self-help books are two-way streets, after all. Relationships. So be honest here, and ask yourself the following question. Is getting filthy rich still your goal above all goals, your be-all and end-all, the mist-shrouded high-altitude spawning pond to your inner salmon?

In your case, fortunately, it seems to be. Because you have spent the last few years taking the essential next step, learning from a master. Many skills, as every successful entrepreneur knows, cannot be taught in school. They require doing. Sometimes a lifetime of doing. And where money-making is concerned, nothing compresses the time frame needed to leap from my-shit-just-sits-there-until-it-rains poverty to which-of-my-toilets-shall-I-use affluence like an apprenticeship with someone who already has the angles all figured out.

The master at whose feet you metaphorically squat is a middle-aged man with the long fingers of an artist and the white-tufted ear hair of a primate resistant to lethal tympanic parasites. He is quick to smile and slow to laugh, and although the skin has begun to sag on his wiry forearms, his sinews remain supple. He owns several secondhand cars, none of them large enough to attract attention, and is habitually to be seen alone in a backseat, immersed in a newspaper, while a driver and sharp-eyed guard ride in front. He cannot himself drive, having come late and suddenly into his prosperity, but he has other offsetting and more lucrative talents, not least his superb numeracy and his keen sensibility for font.

He sits now in a small, windowless room in his factory, an art deco bungalow that has been converted surreptitiously into a manufacturing facility, its boundary wall raised for seclusion in precisely the same manner as those of neighboring private residences. Despite his success, or rather, you have concluded, underpinning it, he oversees the counting of his money himself.

You stand in line, waiting your turn, your pockets bulging with cash and chits of paper bearing mnemonic aids scrawled so illegibly as to be virtually encrypted. When his accountant gestures with his head for you to proceed, you hand over your take and orally present your breakdown, both of which are checked against past figures and inventory records.

"Sales are up," you conclude.

"Like everybody's," the accountant says deprecatingly.

"Mine more than most."

Your master mentions one of your customers. "Last month you said he didn't see a market for tuna."

You nod. "That's what he said."

"What changed?"

"I gave him a few free cans."

"We don't give anything for free."

"I paid for them. Personally."

"I see. And?"

"He sold them. Fast. Now he's a believer."

The accountant enters some numbers into his laptop. Your master scrutinizes the result. He grunts and the accountant returns to you a small portion of the bills you

brought in. This is your compensation, determined by adding together a notional fixed salary, a percentage commis-
sion, and a variable kicker based on how well your master
feels business is doing and you are doing within it. You try
to gauge the amount by the thickness of the wad and the colors of its constituent notes as you shove it into your pocket.
You will count it later.

You are about to leave when your master tells you to ride
with him, an unusual and worrisome request. You follow
him to his car, where he takes out his phone and dials as he
instructs his driver to drive. His guard watches you closely
in the rearview mirror.

Your master conducts his telephonic conversation in a
rural dialect that he does not realize you, whom he pre-
sumes to be a city fellow, understand fluently. Even if your
master knew this, however, it would not concern him. He
employs the dialect not for privacy but because it puts
at ease the supplier he has on the line. Your master has
spent time in many of the small towns in the region that
forms the economic hinterland to your metropolis, and his
chameleon-like ability to match his speech to his surroundings has often worked to his advantage. He would likely be
proud of it, if he were the sort of man who was proud of such
things. But he is too practical for that.

You sit in silence as your master discusses at length

stock movements and delivery dates. The car approaches the outskirts of the city, passing the disinterred earth and linear mounds of vast middle-class housing developments. Rows of electricity poles rise in various stages of completion, some bare, some bridged by taut cables, occasionally one from which wires dangle to the ground.

When your master hangs up he asks what you think of a colleague.

"I think he's good," you say.

"The best?"

"One of."

"Was he stealing from me?"

Everyone steals, at least a little. But you say, "He's not crazy."

"Where was he today?"

"I didn't see him."

He snorts. "You won't be seeing him."

The flatness of your master's tone feels like the side of a blade.

You keep your voice steady. "Yes, sir."

"You understand me?"

"Yes."

The car stops and your master indicates that you are to get out. You do so and halt. You imagine the guard staring at your back. You make no sudden movements, keep your hands in plain view. Only when the car drives off do you turn around, standing at the side of the road and waiting in the heat for a passing bus.

On your return journey you find yourself squeezed against a window by the bulk of an overweight and therefore clearly prosperous vegetable farmer whose clan has recently made the first of a lucrative series of sales of their communal land to a refrigerator assembly plant looking to expand its warehousing space. He wears a gold-plated watch and a thick gold ring set with three uncut rubies the brown-black color of coagulated blood. He does not yet own a car. But that will of course change.

Your city is enormous, home to more people than half the countries in the world, to whom every few weeks is added a population equivalent to that of a small, sandy-beached, tropical island republic, a population that arrives, however, not by outrigger canoe or lateen-sailed dhow but by foot and bicycle and scooter and bus. A limited-access ring road is under construction around the place, forming a belt past which its urban belly is already beginning to bulge, and from which ramps soar and arc off in every direction. Your bus barrels along in the shadow of these monuments, dusty new arteries feeding this city, which despite its immensity is only one among many such organs quivering in the torso of rising Asia.

It is evening by the time you reach home. You wash your body with soap, using a plastic bucket to gather water from an almost impossibly unforthcoming tap, and then dress in the black trousers, white shirt, and black clip-on bow tie arranged for you, along with a plastic security pass, by a former schoolmate who works as a waiter for a catering company. You are excited and nervous, but pleased by your appearance when you glimpse yourself in the mirror of your motorcycle, thinking your garb connotes wealth and class.

Your schoolmate meets you as planned outside the service entrance of a private club that is tonight hosting a fashion show in a pair of pavilions on its expansive lawn. You are both screened for weapons by a uniformed gatekeeper brandishing a hoop-ended metal detector, then perfunctorily motioned through. The shirt you are wearing is a half size too tight at the throat and has begun to chafe when you swallow, but you ignore this discomfort. Your thoughts are on the pretty girl.

You are unable to gain access to the runway pavilion, so you wait at the after-party, or after-reception, rather, the actual after-party, of which you are entirely unaware, being scheduled for much later tonight at the home of the designer whose work is on display. There in the second pavilion, with its temporary bars and tables and plush, semi-recessed lounges, you pace about, hoping she will appear, a tray of drinks balanced on your left hand, precariously, it must be noted, for you have never done this before.

The pretty girl is by now a person of some substance in her industry, even if the term is admittedly an odd one in a profession characterized by its less-is-more physical bias. She is not quite a model of the first rank, but she is well known to photographers and designers and other models, and to readers of picture-laden weekend supplements of local newspapers, a group that because of your abiding desire to see her not infrequently includes you. She earns enough to afford an apartment of her own, a modest but reliable car, and a live-in maid who can cook, which is to say she earns as much as a retail banker her age, and perhaps twice as much as you do, even before the gifts she receives from her multiple, high-churn-rate admirers are taken into account.

She enters now at the side of one of these gentlemen, the handsome although late-blooming and aggressively insecure son of a textile magnate, managing as she walks both to slink and to carry her head with her jaw aligned precisely parallel to the floor, creating thereby an effect of imperious carnality that this year is widely sought after.

You do not know how to attract her attention, and for a moment you are gripped by despair, this venture seeming foolish and doomed to failure. But she is as alert as ever, her laconic expression notwithstanding, and she notices the stare of an out-of-place man in his late twenties with something familiar about him. She returns your gaze at once. Detaching herself from her companion, she approaches.

"Is that you?" she asks.

You nod and find yourself swept up in an embrace. The length of her body presses against yours, embarrassing you, this being a public place, but thrilling you as well. Her touch recalls a moonlit rooftop. When she kisses you on the cheek in plain view of all of these hundreds of people, you wonder if she might still be yours.

"I can't believe it," she says.

"It's incredible."

"So you're a waiter now?"

"What? No, I just . . . I borrowed this."

She smiles.

"I'm in business," you explain.

"Sounds mysterious."

"Sales, actually. I make a lot of money."

"I'm happy to hear that."

She glances around. The two of you are garnering considerable interest because such an enthusiastic meeting of a model and a waiter is unusual, and also because you are on the verge of dropping your tray. The pretty girl has no compunction about causing a scene, but she is aware of the

gap in social status between you, and of the questions perhaps beginning to form in the minds of her colleagues and
clients.

"Here," she says, "put that down and follow me."

She leads you to the main pavilion, past the now-
abandoned runway, and out a backstage entrance, shaking
her head at a security official who bars your way. She waves
hello to a small knot of people from the fashion world, but
otherwise the two of you are alone under the starless sky. A
hot breeze, gently perfumed with diesel, tugs at your clothing. She lights a cigarette and looks you over.

"You've grown up," she says.

"So have you."

"Do you still watch movies?"

"Not that much. Sometimes."

"I'm an addict. I go to sleep in front of the DVD player
every night."

"Every night?"

She raises an eyebrow and smiles inscrutably. "Not every
night. Often. When I'm alone."

"I live with my father. Well, he lives with me. But I have
my own place now."

"Are you married?"

"No. Are you?"

She laughs. "No. I'm not sure I'm the type men marry."

"I'd marry you."

"You're adorable. Maybe I meant I'm not the type men should marry."

"Why not?"

"I change."

"Everybody changes."

"When I change, I let myself change."

"I know. You wanted to leave the neighborhood and now you've done it. You're famous."

"And you?"

"I want to be rich."

She laughs again. "It's that simple?"

"Yes."

"Well, tell me when you are."

"I will. But I don't have your number anymore."

She gives you her phone and you dial yourself, letting it ring twice and saving it under her name. The glow of her cigarette has reached the filter.

"I should get inside," she says.

"I'll call you."

"I know. Take care of yourself."

She kisses you afresh on the cheek, placing her hand at the small of your back. You feel the graze of her breasts against your chest, and then she is gone.

As the pretty girl rejoins her world, she finds her poise

somewhat undermined by your encounter. You are like a living memory and she, who is implacably resistant to remembering, is unsettled by you. Your manner of speech, even though it has evolved in the decade since the two of you last spoke, still carries the cadences of how she once spoke, more than the cadences, the perspectives, the outlook of the neighborhood she once belonged to, a neighborhood she is glad to have fled and to which she does not want to return, even for a moment, even in passing. She tries to focus on her companion, the textile scion, but she is blurry at first, not entirely present, and this alarms her to the extent that she makes a conscious and ultimately successful effort to clear her mind.

You call her that night but she does not answer. You try again the following day with the same result. Later in the week you get hold of her, finally, yet she is distracted, busy getting ready for a shoot. Occasionally thereafter, when you manage to speak with her, you are able to have a brief conversation, but she is always occupied when you suggest meeting. You find this perplexing, and consider how best to proceed. You do not know much about women, but you know a fair bit about sales, and it is apparent to you that this is a case when you must let the customer seek you out, lest you devalue your product completely. So you wait. And she does call. Not often. Not even every month. But sometimes, and usually late in the evening, after she has watched a film, and her voice is languid with impending sleep, and perhaps with alcohol as well, and she speaks to you softly for a few wonderful minutes from the comfort of her bed. She does not invite you over, or propose an encounter elsewhere, but she keeps in touch with you and your life, and this, while at times quietly painful, gives you a measure of hope.

At work you join the scramble for your former colleague's accounts. One prospect rejects your advances, but you have internalized the principle of perseverance and accordingly you revisit him the following season. The man in question runs a shop in a formerly desirable residential area near a much-revered tomb, now choked with traffic by day and scented with marijuana by night.

You arrive on your motorcycle with the strap of your satchel slung bandolier-style across your chest. Your target sits behind the cash register.

"I'm not interested," he says.

"You were before."

"What happened to the other one?"

"I replaced him."

"I didn't trust him."

"You should be happy then."

"I don't trust you either."

He shouts at his assistant, who has knocked over a stack

of breakfast cereal boxes. You glance at the shelves. They are stocked with a mix of foreign and domestically produced goods, foodstuffs mainly, but also cleaning supplies, light-bulbs, cigarettes, and, unexpectedly, a pair of unboxed air conditioners.

You point to the last. "You sell those?"

"They're used. There's demand for them."

You open your satchel and slowly tap half a dozen cans and bottles down on his counter. "Tuna." Tap. "Soup." Tap. "Olives." Tap. "Soy sauce." Tap. "Ketchup." Tap tap tap. "Ly-chee juice." Tap. "All imported."

"I already have all this."

"I know. That's why I'm showing these to you. How much are you paying?"

He looks at you with disgust. "Tell me this. Why are you cheaper?"

"We're a big outfit."

He sneers. "You? I'm sure."

"Our owner has contacts at customs. He gets stuff through without paying duty."

"So does everybody else."

"Why don't you want a good deal?"

"Because I don't like good deals I don't understand."

"It's not stolen."

"I'm not buying it."

"Really, it's not stolen."

"You think I'm deaf?" He spits on the floor at your feet. "Get out."

"There's no reason for . . ."

"Get out, dirty pimp motherfucker."

You stare at him, taking in his potbelly, his flimsy little mouth, his weak, breakable wrists. But you are also aware he keeps his right hand low, under the counter, out of sight. And you sense shoppers taking notice, his assistant lingering at the entrance, passersby pausing outside. Mobs form quickly in these insecure times, and mobs can be merciless. You stand your ground for a moment. Then you garrote your anger, pack your samples, and leave without another word.

"I know all about your scam," he yells out behind you.

You try not to dwell on this incident as you ride back home through the still, smoky dusk. Your costs are low because your master sources recently expired goods at scrap prices, erases the expiry date from the packaging, and reprints a later date instead. This is not as simple as it sounds, there being a number of tricks to removing ink unnoticeably and requiring great attention to detail in the printing process. Products do have built-in safety margins, and inventory turnover in the city is usually high, so for the most part there should be limited risk to consuming what you sell. You are simply increasing the efficiency of the market, ensuring goods that would otherwise be wasted find buyers at reduced price points. You have never heard of anyone dying as a result.

Your work is a far cry from your father's simple trade, but despite your misgivings, you would not consider changing places with him, not at his prime, when he traveled to and from his employer's premises in generally good spirits and good health, and certainly not now, when he is easily exhausted and can no longer stand in the kitchen for more than an hour at a stretch. He has secured a job with a couple returned from abroad who do not like having servants in the house. He wheezes his way over to them every second morning, as they are leaving for work, cooks and refrigerates their dinner for two nights, and takes a bus home by midday. In the afternoons and on alternate days he recovers from his exertions.

The pair of you have moved to slightly larger accommodations, and you have told your father he no longer needs to earn a wage. But he does not desire to be a burden, and in any case he feels employment is the natural state of a man. He would do more if he could, but he cannot.

Your father suffers from a broken heart, both literally and figuratively. He misses your mother intensely, yearning for her even more after her passing than ever during her life. Also his genes and the cholesterol-laden cuisine he has prepared and eaten in wealthy homes for decades have conspired to give him recurring bouts of angina. The damage to his muscle tissue is now irreversible, and although episodes of actual pain are brief, there is no escaping the pressure on his chest or his shortness of breath.

His faith is strong and idiosyncratic, manifesting itself in prayer, visits to shrines, religious music, and sacred verses written on paper and worn as amulets. All of these comfort him. He fears death, but not terribly so, and he awaits the opportunity to be reunited with his beloved much as certain young girls await, with a trepidation that does not quite exceed their longing, the loss of their virginity.

You find him lying on his cot, listening to a tinny yet soulful voice on a battery-powered radio because the electricity is gone and with it the power for your television. He is covered in a shawl, despite the heat, and he sweats lightly from his forehead. You bring him a cup of water and sit beside him, and he pats your hand, his callused palm leathery and almost soft. He whispers a benediction and breathes it into the air, spreading his hopes for you with a contraction of the lungs.

SIX

WORK FOR YOURSELF

LIKE ALL BOOKS, THIS SELF-HELP BOOK IS A CO-creative project. When you watch a TV show or a movie, what you see looks like what it physically represents. A man looks like a man, a man with a large bicep looks like a man with a large bicep, and a man with a large bicep bearing the tattoo "Mama" looks like a man with a large bicep bearing the tattoo "Mama."

But when you read a book, what you see are black squiggles on pulped wood or, increasingly, dark pixels on a pale screen. To transform these icons into characters and events, you must imagine. And when you imagine, you create. It's in being read that a book becomes a book, and in each of a million different readings a book becomes one of a million different books, just as an egg becomes one of potentially a million different people when it's approached by a hard-swimming and frisky school of sperm.

Readers don't work for writers. They work for themselves. Therein, if you'll excuse the admittedly biased tone, lies the richness of reading. And therein, as well, lies a pointer to richness elsewhere. Because if you truly want to become filthy rich in rising Asia, as we appear to have established that you do, then sooner or later you must work for yourself. The fruits of labor are delicious, but individually they're not particularly fattening. So don't share yours, and munch on those of others whenever you can.

In your case you've set up a small business, a workhorse S in the thunderous economic herd of what bankers and policy makers call SMEs. You operate out of a two-room rented accommodation you once shared with your father. Two rooms struck you as a well-earned luxury when he was alive. Now, were it not for the needs of your firm, they would have struck you as wasteful, and disconcerting besides, for even though you are a man in his mid-thirties, you have only recently been introduced to the types of silences that exist in a home with one occupant, and emotionally you stagger about this new reality like a sailor returned to land after decades at sea.

It is shortly before dawn. You sit alone on the edge of a cot that used to sleep your parents, rubbing the dreams from your skull as you listen to an oversexed neighbor-hood rooster crowing in his rooftop cage. You breakfast at a kiosk festooned with the logos of a global soft-drink brand, sipping tea and dipping your fingers into a plate of chickpeas. You are known to many of the men around you, and they nod in greeting, but you are not beckoned into any of the conversations taking place. No matter. Your mind is on the day's work ahead, and as you chew and swallow you barely notice the tethered goat at your feet, with its jaunty, peroxide-bleached forelock, or the battle-scarred, toe-long beetle winding its way to a promising cat carcass.

You have used the contacts with retailers you forged during your years as a non-expired-labeled expired-goods salesman to enter the bottled-water trade. Your city's ne-glected pipes are cracking, the contents of underground water mains and sewers mingling, with the result that taps in locales rich and poor alike disgorge liquids that, while for the most part clear and often odorless, reliably contain trace levels of feces and microorganisms capable of causing diarrhea, hepatitis, dysentery, and typhoid. Those less well-off among the citizenry harden their immune systems by drinking freely, sometimes suffering losses in the process, especially of their young and their frail. Those more well-off have switched to bottled water, which you and your two employees are eager to provide.

Your front room has been converted into a workshop-cum-storage depot. There, in sequence, are a pipe bringing in tap water, a proscribed donkey pump to augment the sputtering pressure from outside, a blue storage tank the size of a baby hippopotamus, a metal faucet, a lidded cooking pot, a gas-cylinder-fired burner to boil the water, which you do for five minutes as a general rule, a funnel with a cotton sieve to remove visible impurities, a pile of used but well-preserved mineral-water bottles recovered from restaurants, and, finally, a pair of simple machines that affix tamper-resistant caps and transparent safety wrapping atop your fraudulent product.

You are leaning over your technician as he conducts an experiment.

"It stinks," you say.

He shrugs. "It's fuel."

"It'll make our water smell like a motorcycle's wet fart."

He lowers the flame. "Now?"

"Too much soot. Turn it off."

You look at the portable petrol stove he has borrowed, dull brass and round as the base of an artillery shell. A shortage of natural gas has yet again brought your operation to a standstill. Petrol, had it worked, might have been an affordable stopgap. But it has not worked. So you try to think of other options as you play with the thread around your neck, fingering the key to your bedroom, where sit your client list and register, a modest pile of cash, and an unlicensed revolver with four chambered rounds.

Your technician scratches his armpit pensively. "Maybe we skip the boiling today," he suggests.

"No. We don't boil, we don't sell." You know quality matters, especially for fakes. Shops would stop buying if their customers began falling sick.

Your technician does not question your decision. He is a bicycle mechanic by background, untrained in the nuances of business, which is why he works for you, and also because, as the father of a trio of little girls and the youngest son of a freelance bricklayer who died of exposure sleeping rough at too advanced an age, he values a steady income.

Were, uncharacteristically, your technician to press you to reconsider, you would likely respond by falling silent, waiting for the pause to grow uncomfortable enough for him to glance in your direction. You would then meet his gaze, holding his eyes until he flicked them floorward and increased the curvature of his spine, gestures which, among teams of humans as among packs of dogs, signify one mammal's submissiveness to another. Mercifully, however, you probably would not sniff his anus or inspect his genitals.

Your runner arrives, announcing the good news that a nearby depot will be refilling gas cylinders for an hour later this afternoon, and also bringing with him the aroma of food, fried-bread lunch rolls sweating translucent their newspaper wrappings. The three of you eat together in fellowship, chatting among yourselves like siblings, which in a way you are, since these two are your clansmen, distant relatives bound by blood, and so yes, like siblings, except of course that when you tell these siblings to finish quickly, they must and do obey.

After the meal, you head to the depot to get in line. Your conveyance is a micro pickup truck older than you are, the side panels of its rear bed holed through in intricate, rusted filigree, but its noisy two-stroke engine rebuilt and reliable. You are at an intersection when your phone rings. Seeing who it is, you pull over, kill the motor, and answer.

"Are you free for dinner?" the pretty girl asks.

Her voice shifts your sense of place, rendering your immediate surroundings less substantial.

"Yes," you say.

"You don't need to know when?"

"Oh. When?"

"Tonight."

You smile, hearing her smile. "Yes, I figured."

"I'm in town. You can come to my hotel."

That evening you get a haircut, opting for a buzz, which the barber claims is both the rage these days and guaran-

teed to flatter a man as fit as yourself. You purchase extrava-
gantly priced tight jeans and a nylon jacket with the words
"Man Meat" on the back from a boutique with impressive
cars parked outside. At home you conclude the jeans are too
short and you rush to swap them for a longer pair, but the
assistant looks you over and, without pausing her online
chat on the shop's computer, refuses on the grounds that you
have removed the tags.

You decide to wear them in any case, unfastening their
top button, concealed beneath your belt, and pulling them
lower on your hips. They squeeze up a small roll of your
flesh, a mini-potbelly, and you wonder if it was a mistake to
buy them. A fortnight's wage outlay for two items of clothing does seem fiendishly unbalanced. But you are getting
late, so now you must speed on to your rendezvous.

The hotel is the city's most exclusive, its old wing temporarily closed and scaffolded since a massive truck bomb
shattered windows and ignited fires inside, but its new
wing, sitting farther from the street, already repainted and
open for business.

After the attack, given the importance of the hotel as a
meeting place for politicians and diplomats and business-
people, and also because of its significance as the outpost of
a leading international chain, a bridge with lofty, illumi-
nated blue signage to the outside world, it was decided to

push the city away, to make the hotel more of an island, insofar as that is possible in a densely packed metropolis such as this. Two lanes formerly intended for traffic have accordingly been appropriated on all sides. The outer of these is fenced with concrete bollards and filled with waist-high anti-vehicular steel barriers, like sharp-edged jacks from the toy room of some giant's child, forming thereby a cross between a dry castle moat and a fortified beach meant to resist armored invasion. The inner lane, meanwhile, features gates, speed bumps, ground-mounted upward-looking CCTV cameras, and sandbag-reinforced wooden pillboxes the color of petunias.

Around this citadel, constricted and slow, traffic seethes. Bicyclists, motorcyclists, and drivers of vehicles with three wheels and four maneuver forward, sometimes bumping, sometimes honking, sometimes rolling down windows and cursing. Every so often their slow crawl gives way to a complete standstill as space is cleared for a bigwig to pass, and then looks of resignation, frustration, and not infrequently anger can be seen. It is from this snarled horde that, nearing the first checkpoint, you seek to detach yourself and enter.

The guard glances at your ride and asks what you want.

"I want to go inside," you say.

"You? Why?"

"I'm meeting someone for dinner."

"Really."

He calls over his supervisor. The taillights of a sleek, gleaming chariot, bearing perhaps a senator or tribune or centurion, flash red as it navigates through the search stations ahead. The supervisor tells you to reverse. He is younger than you, shorter than you, and flimsier than you. But you bite down on your pride, flanked as you are by submachine guns, and plead with him. After a phone call to the pretty girl and a painstaking examination of your diminutive workhorse you are grudgingly permitted to proceed, but only to the secondary parking lot in the rear, from where you must walk.

It is said that in this hotel foreign women swim publicly in states of near nakedness and chic bars serve imported alcohol. You see no sign of such things, maybe because you halt in the lobby, or maybe because in your excitement you are focused on locating the pretty girl. She walks towards you now, high on her wedges, smiling coolly, her hair almost as close-cropped as yours.

She is a visitor to your city, having moved several years ago to an even larger megalopolis on the coast. Her modeling career has plateaued, or perhaps peaked is a better word, since even though the rates she commands remain good, her assignments are declining rapidly in frequency. She is trying therefore to transition to television, and has become a minor actress, minor for the reason that her acting is poor, with credits consisting mainly of bit parts in dramas and comedies. She could not normally stay at this hotel on a personal trip, but occupancy after the bombing has been so low that she secured a discount of fifty percent.

She kisses you on the cheek and observes you closely as she leads you to the restaurant. She notices, yes, that you are uncomfortable in your newly purchased and over-the-top attire, but also, conversely, that you are no longer uncomfortable in your own skin, there being something more mature about you, a sense of confidence, even of mastery, which you have added along with a few pounds and the odd fleck of gray. You seem to her properly a man, not a boy, although pleasingly your eyes have retained their animation, which of course she cannot know, even if she does suspect, owes a great deal to being at this moment in her presence.

You are seated by the headwaiter, who recognizes her and selects a table that maintains a pretense of being out of the way while ensuring she will be widely seen. He is rewarded with a nod from the pretty girl, and he unfolds your napkins personally, handing her hers with a slight bow, not presuming, as he does with yours, the right to place it in her lap.

"You look good," she says to you.

"So do you."

Indeed she does. As with the sun, you have always found it difficult to gaze upon her directly, but tonight you control your instinct to glance away, attempting instead to balance on that crumbly ledge between staring and shiftiness. What you see is a woman little changed by the years, not, obviously, because this is true, your first meeting having been half your lifetimes ago, but rather because your image of her is not entirely determined by her physical reality.

Tonight she wears a yellow spaghetti-strapped top that accents her collarbones and the knuckled indentation of her sternum, along with a single bangle of polished mahogany. A shawl covers the rim of her bag, and she reaches below it to retrieve a bottle of red wine, which she twists open with a sound like the snapping of a twig. You note a hint of uncertainty in her expression, and then it is gone.

"Have you been here before?" she asks.

"No, it's my first time."

She smiles. "So?"

"It's unbelievable."

"I remember my first time. The knives were so heavy, I thought they were silver. I stole one."

"Are they really silver?"

She laughs. "No."

"What else have you seen like that, amazing things regular people don't get to see?"

She pauses, surprised by the stance of your question, the almost-forgotten, for her, terrain of wonder and lowliness it squats upon.

"Snow," she says, grinning.

"You've seen snow?"

She nods. "In the mountains. It's like magic. Like pow-dered hailstones."

"Like what's inside a freezer."

"When it's on the ground. When it's falling, it's like feathers."

"Soft?"

"Soft. But it gets wet. If you walk around in it, it hurts."

You envision her sauntering through a white valley, a mansion in the distance. The headwaiter returns and ties a striped cloth around your bottle, discreetly hiding all but its neck from view.

"What about you?" she asks, refilling your glasses. "What is this business of yours, exactly?"

"Bottled water."

"You deliver it?"

"That too. I make it."

"How?"

You tell her, nonchalantly, omitting mention of the many wrinkles, such as incessant natural gas shortages or long periods when the water pressure is too low and your pump screams idly, unable to fill your storage tank.

"That's brilliant," she says, shaking her head. "And people actually buy it? Just like you were one of the big companies?"

"Just like that."

"You're a genius."

"No." You smile.

"At school everybody always said you were a genius."

"You weren't there often."

"I went for long enough."

You take a drink. "Did you stay in touch with anyone?"

"No."

"Not even your parents?"

"No. They died."

"I know. Mine too. I meant before that."

"Some messages. From them, and later, when I started coming on TV, from relatives. Mostly abuse. Or asking for money."

"So it's just been me."

"Just you." She rests her long fingers on the back of your hand.

You have sampled alcohol only twice before, and never to the point of being drunk, so this sensation of flushed, relaxed glibness is new to you. The two of you eat and chat, occasionally guffawing at volumes disturbing to your fellow diners. Warmth and a craving, a consciousness of your proximity, build within you. But your meal is over too soon, as is the wine, and you are steeling yourself for the evening to end when she says, "I have another bottle in my room. Do you want to come up?"

"Yes."

She tells you the number and asks you to wait a few minutes before joining her. You are confused how to get there exactly, and reluctant to attract the attention of security by asking for directions, but you reason that you must take the elevator, and from there you are able to follow signs in the halls. She opens her door when you knock, brings you inside, and kisses you hard on the mouth.

"I don't have another bottle," she says.

"That's all right."

You hold her, encompassing this familiar, unfamiliar woman, feeling her breathe, tasting the place her words are born. You caress her as you strip her naked. You smooth the curve of her hip, of her jaw. You cradle her pelvis with your palm. No, you are not strangers. You are where you should be, finally, and so you linger.

Sex with you seems transgressive, which heightens her

desire, although she is too preoccupied fully to enjoy the act. There is a whiff of home about you, emotionally, but also physically, in for example your lack of deodorant, and for her home carries with it connotations of sorrow and brutality, connotations that elicit signals from her to you to be punishing, but these you misinterpret, and so they remain unacted upon.

She is passing through a fragile period. Gravity has begun to tug at the arc of her career, and for the first time she earned a fraction last year of what she did the previous. She is aware that her future is shaky, that she could well end up impoverished, aged, and solitary, an elderly lady in a single room, buying rice and flour in bulk once a season, or, no less frightening, the wife of some cocaine-snorting man-child too chronically insecure to appear in his father's head office much earlier than eleven or to stay much later than three, prone to picking up teenage girls at parties in his muscular European limousine and to sobbing unpredictably when drunk.

Lying nude beside you, a used condom on the carpet and a lit cigarette in her hand, she strokes your hair tenderly as you doze. She does not let you spend the night, however. You ask when you will see her next and she is not dishonest, saying she does not know, but to your voiced hope that it be soon, she makes no reply. Afterwards she reclines alone in bed, recalling the comforting sensation of your figures pressed together. She imagines what a relationship with you might be like, whether you could possibly mix with her colleagues and acquaintances in the great city by the sea. She wonders also, as she inhales with shut eyes, the burrowing-termite crackle of paper and tobacco audible, if there will ever arrive a day she is not repelled by the notion of binding herself permanently to a man.

You drive off in a state of agitation, both happy and afraid. But it is the fear that has grown dominant by that weekend, when you take your nephews to the zoo. They long for their monthly outing with their prosperous uncle, for their ride in your truck and the sweets you give them, and on this occasion your longing for their company has been particularly intense as well. Your throat is thick when you collect them, and so you speak little, allowing them to chat among themselves. But in the presence of caged bears and tigers you relax, and you are able to talk normally when it comes time for their camel ride.

Your brother accepts their return with a handshake, and also, wordlessly, the rolled banknotes hidden in your grip. It shamed him initially to receive help from his younger sibling, but not so much anymore, and he no longer insists on telling you over and over the stories of his difficulties as a father in the face of runaway prices, even though those stories remain pressing and true.

Instead he sits you down on his rooftop and asks you about yourself, lighting a joint and sucking a series of shallow puffs into his scrawny chest. The evening sky is orange, heavy with suspended dust from thousands upon thousands of construction sites, fertile soil gouged by shovels, dried by the sun, and scattered by the wind. As usual your brother encourages you to wed, expressing by doing so an abiding generosity, for a family of your own would, in all likelihood, diminish your ability to contribute to the well-being of his.

"My business fills my time," you say. "I'm fine alone."

"No person is fine alone."

Your discussion turns to your sister, whom he has seen on a recent trip to the village and describes as getting old, which does not shock you, though she is only a few years your senior. You are well aware of the toll a rural life exacts on a body. He says she complains often but fortunately her husband is terrified of her, and so her situation is not so bad. She could use some bricks, however, as the mud stacked around her courtyard keeps washing away. You say you will take care of it.

Weeks pass and the pretty girl does not call. You are surprised and unsurprised, unsurprised because this was surely predictable, and surprised because you permitted yourself to hope it might be otherwise. You have learned by now that she will call eventually, but you give up on guessing when that might be.

During this period you come to an important decision. You have amassed some savings, savings you intended to use to buy a resident's bond on your property, not outright title, of course, that being far too expensive, but rather the right to live rent-free in your rooms for a set number of years, after which your landlord must repay your principal. Such an arrangement is a great aspiration for those of modest means, offering as it does security akin to home ownership, temporarily, for the duration of the bond.

In the world of cooks and delivery boys and minor salesmen, the world to which you have belonged, a resident's bond is a rest stop on the incessant treadmill of life. Yet you are now a man who works for himself, an entrepreneur, and one smoky afternoon, as you pass along a road on the outskirts of town, a small plot for let catches your eye, the rump of what was once a larger farm, currently no more than a crumbling shed and a rusty but upon closer examination still functional tube well, and it occurs to you that with the money you have saved, you could instead relocate here and expand your bottled-water operation. Such a course would be risky, leaving you with no savings and no guarantee, should your business fail, of a roof over your head. But risk brings with it the potential for return, and, besides, you have begun to recognize your dream of a home of your own for what it is, an illusion, unless financed in full by cold, hard cash.

The night after you sign the lease, you lie by yourself on the cot that once slept your parents, waiting for exhaustion to push you beyond consciousness. Beside you is your unringing phone. You watch one after another of the ubiquitous, hyper-argumentative talk shows that fill your television, aware that in their fury they make politics a game, diverting public attention rather than focusing it. But that suits you perfectly. Diversion is, after all, what you seek.

SFVEN

BE PREPARED
TO USE VIOLENCE

DISTASTEFUL THOUGH IT MAY BE, IT WAS INEVITA-
ble, in a self-help book such as this, that we would eventually
find ourselves broaching the topic of violence. Becoming
filthy rich requires a degree of unsqueamishness, whether
in rising Asia or anywhere else. For wealth comes from capital, and capital comes from labor, and labor comes from
equilibrium, from calories in chasing calories out, an inher-
ent, in-built leanness, the leanness of biological machines
that must be bent to your will with some force if you are to
loosen your own financial belt and, sighingly, expand.

At this moment, smoke and tear gas coil in the air above
a commercial boulevard. A vinegar-soaked scarf hangs at
your neck as you drive, ready to serve as a makeshift filter
against the fumes. The riot is not ongoing, but neither is it

entirely over, with packs of police out hunting stragglers. Around you broken glass and bits of rubble rest like five o'clock shadow on the city's smooth concrete.

The building at the address you seek has been hit with petrol bombs, its whitewashed colonial facade blackened by smoke. The structure and its interior are by and large fine. But this is not what concerns you as you dismount. What concerns you is the delivery truck in the service lane in front, lying on its side, its engine and undercarriage smoldering. A total loss. There is no need to bother with the extinguisher you have brought, and, after a lingering glance, you wave your mechanic back into your vehicle.

Your mucous membranes ooze on the slow return journey. You roll down your window, hawk deeply, and spit. Your office is adjacent to your factory and storage depot, in the city's outskirts, on one of a thousand and one rutted streets where a few years ago were only fields but now little green can be seen, unplanned development having yielded instead a ribbon of convenience stores, auto garages, scrap-metal dealers, unregistered educational institutes, fly-by-night dental clinics, and mobile-phone top-up and repair points, all fronting warrens of housing perilously unresistant to earthquakes, or even, for that matter, torrential rain.

Here along its spreading rim live many of the recent additions to your city's vast population, some of them born centrally and pressed out by the urban crush, others tossed up from regional towns and villages to seek their fortune, and still others arrived as castaways, fleeing homelands to which in all likelihood they will never return. Here, as well, resides the physical hub of your enterprise. You have thrived to the sound of the city's great whooshing thirst, unsated and growing, water incessantly being pulled out of the ground and pushed into pipes and containers. Bottled hydration has proved lucrative.

Your office, although structurally no different from its narrow, two-story neighbors, is distinguished by its gold-tinted reflective windows, selected by you and striking, to say the least. Stepping into your building, you feel an entrepreneur's pride at observing your people hard at work, hunched over their desks or, as you pass into the corrugated shed out back, over machinery humming in good repair. You built this. But today your pride is mixed with apprehension, reeling as you are from the destruction of the newest addition to your transportation fleet.

You call your accountant into your room and shut the door. Outside, through a tawny pane, you see the top of an overloaded bus snarled in telephone wires. Shouting rises from the street below.

"How bad?" your accountant mumbles.

"Gone."

"Completely?"

You manage to choke off a string of profanities. "I'll need to replace it. Will we be fine for salaries?"

"We have enough cash."

The right half of your accountant's face is stiff from stroke. He is not actually qualified as an accountant, but this does not matter to you. As is customary, you bribe the tax man, and your cooked books serve merely as a starting point for negotiations. What does matter to you is that he be adept with numbers, which he is, having spent decades as a clerk at one of the city's more reputable accountancies.

Your accountant suspects he has not long to live. His visage has already become a mask, its partial rigidity reminding him of his father's in the hours following his father's death, the body bathed but not yet committed to the soil. He often imagines the feeling of tiny blood vessels bursting in his brain, a sensory effervescence, like the prickles of a foot gone to sleep. But he bears his fate for the most part with equanimity. His sons are employed. His daughter is married, to you, a fellow clansman with proper values and excellent prospects. He has therefore completed what a father must most importantly complete, and while the yearning for another chance at youth tempts us all, he is strong enough to hold fast to the truth that time works not that way.

Because you have a lot to do and further because you believe it sends a motivating signal, you depart late this evening. A crescent moon hangs low in the sky, and a pair of flying foxes passes overhead, their giant bat wings thudding through the air. You drive along your customary route, listening to music on the radio.

At an intersection a boyish motorcyclist with delicate, curly hair taps on your window. You lower it to find a pistol pointed at your cheek.

"Get out," he says.

You do. He leads you to the side of the road and tells you to lie facedown in the dirt. Traffic comes and goes, but no one stops or pays any attention. The smell of parched soil fills your nostrils. He places the muzzle against your neck, where your spine meets the base of your skull, and twists it from side to side, grinding. It presses painfully into skin and bone.

"You stupid mother's cock," he says, his voice high-pitched, almost prepubescent. "You think you can buttfuck your betters?"

Your lips move but no sound emerges. You feel phlegm hit your scalp, neutral in temperature and thick like blood.

"This is a warning, sisterfucker. You only get one. Remember your place."

He walks to his motorcycle and rides off. You do not stand

until he is gone. You perceive a sharp discomfort in your upper vertebrae and notice that your car door has remained ajar, the engine idling this whole time. You pop open the glove compartment. Your revolver. Useless.

The ultimatum you have just received comes from a wealthy businessman, part of the city's establishment, who among other things owns a rival bottled-water operation, and onto whose turf you have begun to expand. He is powerful and well connected. So you are frightened, but not only frightened, you are also angry, seethingly furious, both emotions combining to cause you to tremble as you drive, and to think, over and over, while fighting a rising sense of dread, I'll show that fucker, I'll show him.

How you will show him, though, remains unclear.

You pull up at your home, a newly constructed townhouse in an unfinished, mid-price development, one of a choice of four designs repeated in multiple blocks of twelve. The trees on your street are still saplings, knee high, bound to wooden stakes for support against the wind. When your wife lets you in, she looks at you with concern and asks what on earth happened. You say it is nothing, perhaps something you've eaten. Later that night she hears you vomit in the bathroom.

Having recently turned twenty, your wife is a little less than half your age. She believes she has married well, the difference in years notwithstanding, your gap being the same as that between her parents. She grew up in better circumstances than you did, but not in circumstances as comfortable as those she currently enjoys. This, she feels, was to be expected, for she has always been regarded a beauty, with pale skin and a wide, sensuous mouth, and in arranged marriages looks such as hers fairly command a price.

In exchange for her assent to the agreement brokered between your accountant and you, she attached two conditions, first that she be allowed to complete her university, a lengthy course in law, and second that she not be tasked with producing any children while studying. She attached these conditions partly because she wanted them fulfilled and partly to test her power. You acceded, and you are honoring them.

She imagined during the negotiations that she was also testing your desire. Of this, however, she is now less sure. For while sex was a daily, sometimes twice-daily, occurrence in the first weeks of your marriage, it quickly subsided to a rhythm of about once a fortnight. She ascribes this to your being a man in his forties, even if her experience of your initial frenzy does leave her in some doubt. Nonetheless, she continues to look up to you, and feels ready for you to spark in her the flames of romantic love, although she has begun to wonder when you will take the time to do so.

The day you texted the pretty girl on her mobile to inform her of your impending wedding, the pretty girl was surprised, given how little you and she had come to speak in recent years, by the strength of her sadness. She had not consciously been aware of her expectation that you would always wait for her, and while her thoughts occasionally alighted upon memories of you, she had no specific plans for further encounters like the evening you shared in the hotel. So she was caught unsuspecting by her sorrow. Still, she texted you back to wish you happiness. And then, as usual, she did her best to master her feelings and buckle down to work.

A popular cooking show on TV has brought the pretty girl considerable success, which is all the more remarkable since she has never been much of a cook. But she packages a sassy, street-talking persona with a spicy nouveau-street cuisine, combining the dialects of her childhood with the skills of her assistant chefs to charming and profitable effect.

She lives alone in an elegant, minimalist bungalow, not far from the sea, reunited with a generous income after a dip in her fortunes. Her fears of a return to poverty have receded. She recognizes that her celebrity was erected on a foundation of appearance, and she is not blind to the reality that appearances shift. But she believes that there are ways to lift celebrity free of its foundations, indeed that beyond a certain point, celebrity, like a cloud, can become seemingly its own foundation, billowing, self-sufficient, resolutely aloft. Unburdened by the commitments of extended monogamy, she dedicates immense time to this goal, to perpetual publicity campaigns, to those who will sustain her future. To, in other words, her viewers.

Among these viewers is your wife, who finds the pretty girl endearing, like a cool aunt, and her recipes simple and tasty. So you often come home to discover the pretty girl talking to your wife in your living room, their eyes locked across the ether, and when you inevitably ask your wife in a brusque tone to change the channel, she does so with a smile, assuming it is because you, a typically macho man, are uninterested in the wonders of the culinary arts.

You make no mention of your gunpoint warning to your wife, but it leads you to request an audience with the local head of an armed faction to which you and other traders in your area pay protection money. You have not personally seen him before, but as a member of the same clan you expect him to agree to a meeting, and indeed he does not keep you waiting for long.

The encounter takes place in a house that is remarkable only for the two men with assault rifles who loiter outside. The faction head sits on a carpet under a slow-moving fan. He rises, shakes your hand with a mangled but healed appendage missing two of its fingers, and watches you appraisingly. Settling yourself beside him, you explain your predicament.

The faction head is inclined to help, first because you will pay, and second because you are kin, and third because he sees you as an underdog and he regards himself as a champion of underdogs, and fourth because the businessman who threatened you belongs to a sect the faction head believes deserving of extermination. But he tells you none of this immediately. Instead he informs you of his decision the next day, having in the meantime, since he is middle management, conferred with his superiors, and also having let you sweat.

You are given a guard for your personal security and an unelaborated verbal guarantee of further measures should the situation escalate. The guard arrives unannounced at your office, so quiet and calm as to be virtually opiated, but with sharp, unsmiling eyes. He is roughly your age though significantly heavier, packing a barrel stomach and four silver teeth. You cannot imagine him a father or a husband, so you do not ask him about his family, and he, for his part, makes no small-talk either. He spends the nights at your home, but even with him outside, in your single and otherwise unoccupied servant quarter, it troubles you to have this man living near your wife.

Whenever he sits in your car, the guard cocks his automatic noisily between his legs, whether for effect or to improve his reaction time or simply out of habit, you are not entirely sure. You wonder if you have made a mistake by engaging him, as the expense is crippling and he makes you uncomfortable besides. But, as you see it, your only alternatives are to ignore the threat, which might be suicidal, or to back down and submit to your rival, which would be unfair and a blow to your pride. Once, as you intentionally drive by the businessman's walled villa, an acre of prime property in an upscale district, you glimpse him through a closing gate power-walking on his lawn. His gray tracksuit and blue hand weights are evocative of a certain type of filmic villain, and this sight steels you in your determination not meekly to surrender.

Your wife knows that something is bothering you, perceiving you to be distant and uncharacteristically irritable, and she recognizes it is not without significance, of course, that her husband has newly retained a guard. She desires to be a comfort, and when her attempts to engage you in conversation fail to elicit an explanation of what is the matter, she takes another tack, proposing that the two of you go out to see a movie, or dine at a restaurant, but you are adamant about spending evenings at home, for security reasons, although you do not tell her this last, not wanting to frighten her.

The imported glossy magazines she reads offer advice on what to do in this situation, how to please your man when he seems unpleased, and so, greatly daring, as your anniversary approaches, she instructs her waxing lady to remove all of her pubic hair, a bracingly painful experience, purchases with the entirety of her month's pocket money an expensive, lacy set of bra and panties, in violet, her favorite color, and waits for you on your bed, semi-undressed, in the glow of flickering candles.

She is unaware that the electricity has gone out, and so is taken aback when you enter the room holding a portable, battery-powered tube light, and you, for your part, are embarrassed at having stumbled in on her unannounced, and so you avert your eyes, muttering an apology, and head straight for the bathroom. When you return she is covered to her chin with a sheet, her eyes big in the dimness, a sense of humiliation washing over her, and yet, when you lie down, she reaches deep within, and, summoning extreme reserves of willpower, places your hand upon her chest and her hand between your legs, and she feels her body swelling and hardening to you, but not yours to her, overcome as you are by exhaustion and stress, and so she turns around and clenches her face against sound and wetness and pretends to go to sleep.

For you the weeks pass in fraught tension, your gaze incessantly flicking around you as you drive, wondering whether you will be attacked, and wondering also what, if anything, your guard will be able to do to protect you. You tell yourself you will not give in to fear, but despite this you begin to cancel visits even to those corporate customers with which your firm has its most lucrative cooler-replenishment contracts. Your business suffers as a result, as your days take on a more and more rigid schedule of early to work, stuck in the office, and late to home.

This routine is initially broken not by an act of violence but by the death of your sister. The arrival of the monsoon has brought with it sudden floods, and while the houses of your ancestral village, through a blessing of topography, have mostly been spared, resultant pools of stagnant water have bred armies of disease-carrying mosquitoes. Your sister is killed by dengue, her high fever relenting, and briefly offering false hope, before internal bleeding starves her organs and causes them to fail.

You travel on a series of lurching buses with your brother and his sons, themselves now nearly men, not reaching your destination until the following evening because of rain-damaged roads and bridges. The funeral has been delayed to make possible your presence, and thus you are able to see your sister one final time, a woman old without having been so long on this world, her white hair sparse and front teeth missing, the flesh of her face sunken to her bones, as if deflated by the passing of her life.

Looking at your brother, you observe that he too has aged, though even as a young man he tended not to seem young, and you wonder how you must appear to your nephews. You offer your prayers at the flower-strewn mound of earth that caps your sister's resting place, and you give the money you have brought to her husband and children. Death in the village, being common, is handled in a matter-of-fact manner, and after the first few days you witness no wailing, even if a tear is shed by your eldest niece when she bends to allow you to place a palm on her head as you depart.

You left your wife behind in the city, a decision experienced by her as hurtful, despite your claim that the journey would be too arduous because of the floods. She finds it shocking you did not want her present on such an important occasion, unknowing that your true motivation was your wish to conceal somewhat the shabbiness of your origins.

As you return, slowly, through innumerable blockages, dismounting to help heave vehicles free of treacherous mud, you are reminded again of the yawning gap that exists between countryside and city, of the intensity with which here eyes follow a goat, the sole survivor of its swept-off herd, while there existence continues largely unchanged.

Later that week the boyish gunman is once more given instructions to encounter you. He washes and dresses as usual, listening to movie songs on a promotional soda-can-shaped radio and shaving above his upper lip in the aspiration of one day provoking a mustache. His mother and sister bid him good-bye. He is low on funds and so he purchases only a small quantity of petrol for his motorcycle and a single loose cigarette. He chooses an intersection on your route with a giant billboard advertising antibacterial soap, and waits, smoking, a new habit good for making him forget that he is hungry. His phone beeps to inform him you are on your way.

The gunman's mind lingers on a T-shirt he had been wanting, purple, with a psychedelic hawk, but it was gone when he passed by the store today, and the shopkeeper said it was sold. He wishes he had been able to buy it. He should have borrowed the money. There is a girl with dimples from his neighborhood he has not had the courage to speak to, and she never seems to notice him, but he is sure she would have in that T-shirt.

You too are thinking of a woman as you approach the intersection, recalling the imaginary games you once played with your sister. In front of you a truck is hauling a shipping container, and its brakes start to hiss as it decelerates. Amidst this noise you see the gunman striding towards you, and you turn to your guard, but he has already understood. Your guard shoots thrice through your windscreen. The gunman falls. You are ready to flee but your guard opens his door and steps out onto the street. One of the bullets has dislodged a curly-haired piece of cranium. It rests not far from where the gunman lies, struggling to breathe. Your guard fires several rounds into his face and chest and snaps a photo with his mobile phone. Reoccupying his seat, he tells you to drive, and when you do not seem to understand, he repeats himself, and you quickly obey.

You stop on a deserted road and your guard uses the socket wrench from your tire-change kit to smash your damaged windscreen, cracking it like an eggshell. He pushes it free from inside the car, employing both feet, and carries it to a pile of rubbish. A humid breeze ruffles your collar as you continue home, and that night you lie with your revolver under your bed, unable to sleep. You wonder what will happen now, if you will suffer violent retribution, a prospect made much more concrete by your vivid recollections of the gunman's slaying.

But you are subsequently informed by the faction head that the photo has been transmitted, along with a written communication, to the businessman, and a cessation of his threats against you has been agreed upon. You do not know whether entirely to believe this, whether some larger scheme is instead playing itself out, but your guard is taken away, and so you recommence after months to move about alone, hoping for the best, and also putting your affairs in order, in case you are mistaken.

Your business prospers, and soon the entire incident becomes, if not a distant memory, at least not a pressing concern. You work long hours, returning late to your wife, and focus on your immediate tasks. You think from time to time about the pretty girl, and she thinks about you, but she does not communicate, holding back whenever she feels the impulse to do so, not wanting to interfere in your happiness with your wife, and you do the same, and for the same reason. But even unconnected in this way, the pretty girl does interfere, for you are unable to open yourself to your wife fully, seeing reminders of the pretty girl in her, as though the pretty girl has become your archetypal woman, of which your wife can only be a copy, and hearing in your wife's laughter and feeling between your wife's legs echoes of the pretty girl, painful echoes that cause you to shut yourself off and keep away.

You try to compensate materially, buying your wife an expensive necklace, nothing when compared to those worn by heiresses and celebrities, of course, but still of a modest splendor neither she nor you has previously possessed, and this gift pleases her, but her hope that your gesture will be accompanied by the genuine tenderness she craves soon fades, and the necklace stays in its box, unworn, on all but the odd night or two a year.

Increasingly, your wife comes to find herself unsettled by the attention she receives from many young men at her university, and by her own desire sometimes to respond, always quickly repressed since she has been raised to believe in the inviolability of marriage, and so she starts to dress more modestly, and even to cover her hair when she leaves the house, establishing thereby a barrier between her and the covetousness around her, and a degree of inner calm.

Lying beside her in your bed, untouching, a newly installed little generator rumbling downstairs as it shields you both from electrical outages, and your head on a towel because age and postural problems have combined to give you a recurring stiffness of the neck, it does not occur to you that your wife's love might be slipping from your grasp, or that, once it is gone, you will miss it.

EIGHT

BEFRIEND A
BUREAUCRAT

NO SELF-HELP BOOK CAN BE COMPLETE WITHOUT taking into account our relationship with the state. For if there were a cosmic list of things that unite us, reader and writer, visible as it scrolled up and into the distance, like the introduction to some epic science-fiction film, then shining brightly on that list would be the fact that we exist in a financial universe that is subject to massive gravitational pulls from states. States tug at us. States bend us. And, tirelessly, states seek to determine our orbits.

You might therefore assume that the most reliable path to becoming filthy rich is to activate your faster-than-light marketing drive and leap into business nebulas as remote as possible from the state's imperial economic grip. But you would be wrong. Entrepreneurship in the barbaric wastes furthest from state power is a fraught endeavor, a constant battle, a case of kill or be killed, with little guarantee of success.

No, harnessing the state's might for personal gain is a much more sensible approach. Two related categories of actor have long understood this. Bureaucrats, who wear state uniforms while secretly backing their private interests. And bankers, who wear private uniforms while secretly being backed by the state. You will need the help of both. But in rising Asia, where bureaucrats lead, bankers tend to follow, and so it is on befriending the right bureaucrat that your continued success critically depends.

You sit before him now, in his government office, spacious yet dowdy, as such offices often are, with dusty windows, framed portraits of a pair of national leaders, one dead and one alive, and chunky wooden seating in need of reupholstery, which, if reconfigured, could easily accommodate twice as many visitors, and communicates through its weightily inefficient refusal to do so a loud and clear signal of intent. Many bribes were paid to enable this meeting, most importantly to the bureaucrat's personal secretary, without whose assent slots in his calendar seem never to open up, and so here you are, with the head honcho himself, finally able to make your pitch.

The bureaucrat, in violation of nonsmoking regulations, lights an exquisitely expensive gifted cigar from his well-appointed humidor without offering you anything but a cup of tea. He knows your type, self-made, on the rise, and because of his education, family background, and temperament he regards you with disdain, but also with satisfaction, for there is usually more money to be had from supplicants who seek to challenge the status quo than from those who seek merely to maintain it.

You were delivered to him by a sticky web of red tape. Permits denied, inspections failed, meters improperly read, audits initiated, all these scams and hassles you have over the years surmounted by greasing junior and mid-level palms. But you have reached an impasse. Your firm has become fairly aboveboard, at least as far as product is concerned, sterilizing mostly to the accepted standard and bottling under your own name. Yet your expansion into the big leagues, into the mass market of the piped municipal water game, has been stymied. Only state-licensed providers can bid for municipal contracts, and your application for such a license has been turned down. So you have pursued the rejection to its source, this man seated in front of you.

He puffs away, the fingertips of his free hand resting on a file containing your recently dismissed proposal. You drone on about the technical soundness of your candidacy, your capital and expertise, your many satisfied customers. The bureaucrat lets you expend your energy, punch yourself out, presentationally, and when you inevitably fall silent he writes two words on a sheet of paper in the indigo ink of his gold-nibbed fountain pen and pushes them towards you. They are, "How much?"

You are relieved. A hurdle has been crossed and the negotiation can now begin. But you pretend otherwise.

"Sir," you say, "we meet the conditions . . ."

"Have you previously been a municipal vendor?"

"We've been in the water business almost twenty years."

"Have you previously been a municipal vendor?"

"No."

"Are you authorized to be a municipal vendor?"

"Not yet."

"No." He propels a perfect smoke ring with an unhurried flick of his jaw.

"All your requirements have been satisfied."

"All our quantifiable requirements. It is my duty to ensure our unquantifiable requirements are also met. Reputational requirements, for example."

"Our reputation is that we're friendly."

"Good."

You observe him. He is nearer sixty than fifty, and so less than a decade your senior, but with the velvet-cushion new-born grip of a man who has eschewed not merely manual labor and racket sports but even carrying his own briefcase.

He directs, with a tap of his finger, your attention to the piece of paper between you. These days, regrettably, it is difficult to know when a conversation is being recorded. He prefers to keep impropriety inaudible. You make a show of pausing in consideration before inscribing a sum you feign is impressive. The bureaucrat rejects it with a curt shake of his head, scribbling a vastly greater, but reduced, figure. You feel a glow of satisfaction. In not dismissing you out of hand he has slid off his viceroy's throne and into a salesman's stall. You are his buyer, and though you must not squeeze, you have him by his enormous, greedy, and extremely useful balls. You haggle, but magnanimously.

The bureaucrat cannot, however, act without the approval of his political masters, and therefore, the following week, after another meeting with you to fill in the specifics of your arrangement, he dispatches you to the home of a politician familiar to you from TV and newspapers. You are driven by your driver in your hulking and only slightly secondhand luxury SUV. Positioned beside him is a uniformed guard normally employed by you to open and shut the gate of your house. You sit in the back, ostensibly browsing e-mails on your computer, hoping to make a substantial impression.

Fears of terrorism have led the politician to take measures to secure his residence, strong-arming his neighbors
into selling him their properties, erecting a razor-wire-
topped boundary wall far in excess of permissible heights,
and placing illegal barricades at either end of the street.
Police officers mill about on foot, and a heavily armed
rapid-response unit idles in a pickup truck, ready to accompany him on the move. You are allowed to proceed, but
without your vehicle and retainers, much to your disappointment, and you are frisked twice on your way in.

The politician's working environment is structured in
the manner of the courts of princes of old, namely with one
set of waiting rooms for commoners, another for those of
rank, and an inner sanctum occupied by him and a contin-
gent of his advisers. Your transaction is conducted simultaneously with multiple unrelated strands of endeavor, some
public, some personal, and some apparently without purpose, or rather with no purpose other than amusement. An
extended lunch is under way, and so everything happens
to the sounds of chewing and with repeated gestures that
look like multi-fingered snaps but are in reality attempts to
dislodge grease, rice, and bits of edible residue without the
use of water or tissues. None of this surprises you or throws
you off, the bureaucrat having prepared you well, and in any

case your dominant feeling is one of achievement at being with people of such importance.

Your deal is concluded in an uncomplicated, if seemingly whimsical, fashion, the politician asking one of his hench- men for an opinion with a laugh and raised eyebrow, much as he might ask him to assess the desirability of a mid-priced prostitute. A number is thrown out. This is accepted by you with obsequious murmurs and bows of the head, precisely as you have been instructed to do by the bureaucrat. And that is that.

As you drive off, under a beautiful, orange, polluted sky, riding high in your SUV above lesser hatchbacks and motorcycles, you start to hum, only the presence of your employees preventing you from bursting into full-blown song. What a long way you have come. Your offices loom ahead, the entire second floor of a centrally located empo- rium, atop a bustling array of shops. Security men and parking attendants salute you, elevator doors spring apart for your arrival, and your nods to a select few of your man- agers, as you stride by their desks, spark a buzz of chatter. Yes, your meeting was a success.

Your son is delivering an address on the lawn when you get home. It is twilight, a moment adored by mosquitoes, and he wears shorts and a T-shirt, the sight of his bare brown flesh worrying you until he runs over and into your arms, granting you the pleasure of lifting his solid little form, his vertebrae clicking softly as gravity tugs them apart, and sniffing on his skin the synthetic lemon-lime aroma of insect repellent. Your son is a big-cheeked, bowl-haircut-sporting, navel-high orator, and this evening he has assembled about him not just his nanny but the cook and bearer as well, all of whom become markedly more formal in your presence. The boy is subjecting them to a political speech modeled after one he must have seen on TV.

"When I am your leader . . ."

You watch and listen, wishing as always that you had more time with him, that you could take him with you to work or, even better, stay here with him and his toys, and also thinking of your parents, realizing that they must have experienced, half a century ago, the same emotions you feel now, except in their case with more trepidation, for while disease or violence could of course strike down your son, the probability of his early death has, through your attainments, been reduced dramatically.

Interrupting his performance, you charge at him with a roar. He flees into the house, squealing, and you yell that you will eat him up, but you quieten as you pass inside, parked cars on your street having alerted you to an ongoing meeting. Your wife sits with a dozen other women, their heads covered and in several cases their faces too, engaged in heated debate. Your greeting elicits a verbal response from her, but her eyes rest upon your son, and it is he alone she favors with a smile as the two of you proceed upstairs, followed, scooter in hand, by his nanny. The conversation around your wife subsides at this sudden claim on her attention, but resumes with equal vigor when she tilts her head and gestures to her collaborators with upraised palms, as though marshalling some unseen but weighty force, or communicating a deep and shared sense of exasperation, or otherwise supporting a pair of invisible breasts.

It has been five years, the age of your son, since you last entered your wife's body. Intercourse between you had already been infrequent, and only a lucky roll of the biological dice explains why she conceived so quickly after completing her studies and removing her contraceptive coil. Childbirth, however, was less easy. A severe third-degree perineal tear damaged your wife's anal sphincter. With reconstructive surgery and endless hours of physiotherapy, she defeated the resulting incontinence, and she is now free of the diapers she was forced to wear, galling for a woman so young. But you were almost entirely absent from this process, clumsily semi-aware, at best, of the details of her condition. Consumed by your work, made hesitant by your upbringing and gender, and in any case pining for that other woman be-

yond your reach, you readily paid for whatever needed paying for, but did no more.

Yet you have changed with the growth of your son. Medi-
calized, bloody, and enacted to the sound of screaming and
the smell of disinfectant, his birth was like a death. It shook
you. And, slowly, it unlocked forgotten capacities for feeling.
Fatherhood has taught you the lesson that, even in middle
age, love is practicable. It is possible to adore those newly
come into your world, to envision, no matter how late in the
day, a happily entwined future with those who have not
been part of your past. And so, armed with this wisdom, you
are attempting to woo your wife, to build a family on the
strength of the bond that is your son, to win her joy and
smiles and caresses, to entice her back to your side from her
separate bed lying parallel to yours.

But when you began to turn to her again, to try to see her,
as if for the first time, as an adult and a mother and indeed
something wondrous, a warrior, striking in her maturing
beauty and her indefatigable determination, and you sought
to make conversation with her and to stroke her arm and
her cheek and her thigh, you discovered your wife uninterested. She has never shouted at you in anger. In fact, she
continues to exhibit a well-brought-up sympathy for your
age, which, with your litany of minor ailments, ranging
from your spine to your teeth to your knees, has started to

seem further and further removed from her own. But she avoids discussions with you that are not practical in nature, finding troubling your attempts to engage in this manner, as though violative of the terms of your truce. The focus of her attention is elsewhere, on her son, and on her group of religiously-minded activists.

In their company, she conducts herself with a gravity that exceeds her years, enjoying an influential position despite the fact that many of them are her seniors. Her legal training and relative prosperity give her pertinent advantages, of course, but mostly it is her bearing, her self-sufficient fire and evident fearlessness, that others rally to, coupled with her disarming warmth, much sought-after and awarded only to a fortunate few.

You are aware, when she comes tonight, draped in her shawl, to read your son his bedtime story and put him to sleep, that you cling to him not just because of your feelings for the boy, which are powerful and true, but also because in this moment, with your arms around your child, you have something she wants, a precious sensation, and one you simultaneously desire to prolong while feeling sad, even ashamed, of engendering solely in this way.

Hoping it might positively impact your relations with your wife, some months ago you hired one of her brothers into your firm. He joined an already sizable band of kinfolk and clanspeople owing their paychecks to you, many without contributing notably to your enterprise. But from the outset his cleverness and education distinguished him from the others, so much so that you are considering grooming him as a potential deputy.

It is with him, after receiving from the bureaucrat your municipal vendor's license and winning your first contract to augment the public water supply, that you travel to the coast to clear your equipment through customs. The two of you ride together to the airport. A new terminal sits across the runway from its predecessor, in what was formerly cropland but now lies within the ambit of the ring road, surrounded by housing developments, defense installations, slum-subsumed villages, golf courses, and the occasional hotly contested field, still free of construction and sprouting fronds of mustard, wheat, or corn.

Because of a hypertrophying middle class, bulging from the otherwise scrawny body of the population like a teenager's overdeveloped bicep, there has been a surge in air traffic, demand the state carrier simply cannot meet. To get a flight at the time of your choosing you use one of several haphazardly regulated private operators. On board you find it difficult to ignore your jetliner's probable military heritage, manifested among other things in its oddly shaped engine pods and rear-opening ramp, suitable perhaps for embarking howitzers or armored personnel carriers. You have always been fatalistic about flying, but as a father you dislike the idea of permanently leaving your son so soon, a possibility evoked in your imagination by juddering vibrations that roar through the fuselage as you ascend.

Your brother-in-law is visibly excited, pleased to be seated in business class and to be booked into a fancy hotel. He resembles your wife, albeit a plump, squat, mustachioed version of her. He is your wife compressed in height, expanded in depth and width, and masculinized, as though by a computer program in a science museum's digital house of mirrors. He has the same pale complexion and sensuous mouth, the same verbal tics. Without being conscious of it, you have allowed yourself to become fond of him not for the content of his character but for the fidelity of his echo.

As you exit the baggage-claim area at the other end, a blast of hot briny air hits your face, thrilling you, as always, this place being in your estimation linked with money, with the big time. Around you is a crush of people more diverse than those you see at home, their languages more varied, their skin and lips and hair testifying to wider geographic swaths of evolution. They have been pulled to this colossal city by the commerce linked to its port, which straddles the shipping lanes binding rising Asia to Africa, Oceania, and beyond, and also by its gravity, the force exerted by its sheer mind-boggling size.

A limousine whisks you to your hotel, in a prestigious neighborhood, where cluster consulates and the offices of multinationals, united by colonial history and also by relatively easy access to naval evacuation should that be required. High in your room, you gaze out at the sea, mesmerizing to you, a man from the far-off plains, as you watch its fractured surface catch the light, scattered clouds repixelating its colors while speeding overhead. You nibble on tiny chocolates and an assortment of exotic berries, too delicate though to constitute much of a meal, and think, This must be success. In the distance you can make out the docks. There awaits your machinery.

At equal remove, but unknown to you, and in the opposite direction along the coast, is the residence of the pretty girl. She is sitting beside her lap pool, in the shade of a tree, wearing a fawn swimsuit and retro dark glasses while sipping a sugar-free cordial through a bendable straw. She has just returned from a journey through a series of peninsulas and archipelagos, the latest of the monthlong procurement trips she now embarks upon semi-annually, which typically require, for each week of travel, at least two in visa processing.

She and you reconnect on your visit, tangentially at least, through an executive who works in his family's freight-forwarding business by day and is a fixture of the contemporary art and fashion scenes by night. In his office, as he tells you how lucky you are that your bureaucrat intervened with colleagues in customs to speed your goods through import inspections and minimize your demurrage charges, you see on his desk a photo of him at an award ceremony with a group of celebrities. You ask seemingly casually if he knows the pretty girl, and he says, why, yes, as a matter of fact he does.

Through him you learn, for she has not been on TV in some time, that she is well, and indeed busy, running a high-end home furnishings boutique, and also, since he has a keen eye for such things and knows at once your claim of being merely an old acquaintance is less than the entire truth, that she is the lover of a prominent and recently widowed architect.

For you these remarks bring her clearly into focus, even if that focus is a product only of memory and imagination, and you feel strongly, exactly what you are not sure, whether happiness or sadness or neither or both, but strongly, a breath-halting feeling, a sensation, like asthma, of being unable to empty your lungs. Her own response is not dissimilar, when, a few weeks later, the freight forwarder spies her at an afternoon seaside reception and glides up to her, eager to chat, certain she will be more than surprised at the name he is about to let slip, as by a gurgling fart during a passionate embrace.

So the pretty girl discovers that you are a father, the juxtaposition ironic, in a way, though she never desired children, for she has recently entered menopause, and also that your business is flourishing, and further that you continue to have a sexy little something about you, a rustic manliness, a touch of the uncouth, a hip-shaking coarseness common to people from your inland backwater, and so filthily hot and lacking around here. She smiles at this description and asks for more, but decides against divulging the details of her shared past with you, if for no other reason than that she has not discussed it with anyone before, and after all these years it seems unnatural to start. She says only that you and she had a thing, once upon a time.

She herself is tolerably content. Her transition from television chef to designer-kitchen showroom owner to retailer of one-of-a-kind international furniture and expensive bric-a-brac has not been without its moments of difficulty. But now her establishment is humming along nicely, she has an excellent assistant, a well-educated and divorced woman free to accompany and translate for her on her lengthy travels abroad, travels the pretty girl enjoys,

seeing them as adventures, and as for her romantic entan-
glements, well, they may not have been especially fiery of
late, but at least they do persist.

As she speaks of you with the freight forwarder, watching two traditionally clad waiters struggle to reposition a
massive orchid sculpted of ice, you too are watching men
toil away, standing at the construction site of your water-
mining plant with your brother-in-law at your side. Despite
the modest size of your project, he has had hard hats issued
to your employees, an innovation you value because it adds a
veneer of professionalism. Your scalp sweats under this
plastic second skull, the sun bearing down mercilessly, and
rivulets of perspiration sting your eyes and stroke saltily
the corners of your mouth.

Below your feet is the ever-dropping aquifer, punctured
by thousands upon thousands of greedily sipping machine-
powered steel straws. Your installation is not the largest of
its kind, but it is brighter than most others, shiny and pristine and new. Yet, standing there, for an instant you catch a
whiff of something quite inexplicable, or at least you think
you do, a scalding breeze carrying to your nose the blood-
like aroma of rust.

Today your wife will doubtless be intervening with her
women's group to help another beaten spouse or homeless
divorcee or disinherited widow, actions that are all for the

good and have nothing to do with you, but contain a degree of implicit reproach. You shut your eyes, briefly seized by a strange regret, maybe for the delays to this project, or for the state of your marriage, or for becoming so late a father to your son, for being, in all likelihood, destined to overlap too limitedly with the span of his life. But the mood passes. You master yourself, spit a clot of parched sputum into the dirt, and carry on, exhorting your welding crew to make good time.

NINE

PATRONIZE THE
ARTISTS OF WAR

WE'RE ALL INFORMATION, ALL OF US, WHETHER readers or writers, you or I. The DNA in our cells, the bio-electric currents in our nerves, the chemical emotions in our brains, the configurations of atoms within us and of subatomic particles within them, the galaxies and whirling constellations we perceive not only when looking outward but also when looking in, it's all, every last bit and byte of it, information.

Now, whether all this information seeks to comprehend itself, whether that is the ultimate goal to which our universe trends, we obviously don't yet know for certain, though the fact that we humans have evolved, we forms of information capable of ever-increasing understandings of information, suggests it might be the case.

What we do know is that information is power. And so information has become central to war, that most naked of our means by which power is sought. In modern combat, the fighter pilot, racing high above the earth at twice the speed of sound, absorbs different streams of information with each eye, radar reflections and heat signatures with one, say, and the glint of sunlight on distant metal with the other, a feat requiring years of retraining of the mind and sensory organs, a painstaking human rewiring, or upgrade, if you will, while on the ground the general sees his and disparate other contemporary narratives play out simultaneously, indeed as the emerging-market equity trader does, and as the rapid-fire TV remote user and the multiple-computer-window opener do, all of us learning to combine this information, to find patterns in it, inevitably to look for ourselves in it, to reassemble out of the present-time stories of numerous others the lifelong story of a plausible unitary self.

Perhaps no one does this with more single-minded dedication or curatorial ferocity than those at the apex of organizations entrusted with national security. These artists of war are active even when their societies are officially at peace, quests for power being unrelenting, and in the absence of open hostilities they can be found either hunting for ever-present enemies within or otherwise divvying up that booty always conveniently proximate to those capable of wanton slaughter, spoils these days often cloaked in purchasing contracts and share-price movements. To partner in such ventures is to be invited to ride the great armorplated, signal-jamming, depleted-uranium-firing helicopter gunship to wealth, and so it is only natural that you are at this moment considering clambering aboard.

From the perspective of the world's national security apparatuses you exist in several locations. You appear on property and income-tax registries, on passport and ID card databases. You show up on passenger manifests and telephone logs. You hum inside electromagnetically shielded military-intelligence servers and, deep below pristine fields and forbidding mountains, on their dedicated backups. You are fingertip swirls, facial ratios, dental records, voice patterns, spending trails, e-mail threads. And you are one of a pair of suited figures seated in the rear of a luxury automobile now approaching a combat-uniformed MP at an entry checkpoint to your city's cantonment.

This MP has only seconds to determine which vehicles to pull aside for his unit to search. Trucks, buses, and those cars that have three or more exclusively male passengers under the age of fifty are mandatorily inspected. For all others he relies on instinct and also on randomness, predictability being a fatal flaw in any defensive system. He decidedly does not like the looks of you. Wealthy civilians, in his view, are a subcategory of thief. They have robbed this country blind for generations. But wealthy civilians are also likely to have contacts with generals, and so they stand partly outside the otherwise clear five-tier hierarchy of officer, NCO, enlisted man, loyal citizen, enemy. His eyes scan your expression, taking in your calm air of control, and the expressions of your colleague and of your driver. He waves you through.

A series of CCTV cameras observes various stages of your progress through the cantonment. Through their monochromatic optical sensors the expensive metallic finish of your sedan dulls to a ratty gray. Behind you are scenes little changed since independence, images of well-manicured lawns, mess halls with regimental insignia, trees painted waist-high in skirts of white. Homes of the descendants of corps and division commanders abut those of oligarchic commercial magnates, and everywhere is a sense of unyielding order and arboreal grace increasingly atypical of your city, much of the rest of which seethes outside this fortified garrison enclave like some great migratory horde besieging a royal castle.

Another unit of MPs sees you exit the cantonment, and ten minutes later private wardens watch as you pass below the arch that signals the start of an elite housing society marketed, developed, and administered by one of a comprehensive network of military-related corporations. At the headquarters of this enterprise the gaze of a rooftop sniper follows you and the brother-in-law who is your deputy and chief operating officer as you both dismount. Inside, a retired brigadier shakes your hands, leads you to the boardroom, and tells you with proprietary pride about their latest scheme.

"Phase ten is big," he says. "It's bigger than phases one to five put together. Bigger than seven and eight combined. Bigger even than six, and six was huge. Ten is a milestone. A flagship. With ten we're taking it to the next level. Ten will have its own electricity plant. No blackouts in ten."

He pauses, waiting for a response.

"Incredible," your brother-in-law offers. "Unbelievable."

"But that's not all. Other premier housing societies are installing electricity plants. We're rolling them out across all our phases, in all our cities. No, what's going to make ten unique, and why you're here, is water. Water. In ten, when you turn the tap, you'll be able to drink what comes out of it. Everywhere. In your garden. In your kitchen. In your bathroom. Drinkable water. When you enter phase ten, it'll be like you've entered another country. Another continent. Like you've gone to Europe. Or North America."

"Without leaving home," your brother-in-law says.

"Exactly. Without leaving home. You'll still be here. But in a secure, walled-off, impeccably maintained, lit-up-at-night, noise-controlled, perfectly regulated version of here. An inspiration for the entire country, and for our country-men abroad too. Where even the water is as good as the best. World class."

"Fabulous." Your brother-in-law salutes for added em-phasis.

"Can it be done?"

"Yes."

The brigadier smiles. "Right answer. We know it can be done. What we want to know is who can do it. Who can be our local partner. We're setting up a water subsidiary. We'll have top international consultants. But we need someone who can execute, someone with a track record in this city. Which is why you're on our shortlist. It'll be our brand, our face to the public. Naturally. But we can't do it alone, not yet. So there's excellent money to be made working with us, especially while we're getting up to speed."

"We're thrilled to have the chance."

"Are you?" The brigadier looks pointedly in your direction, where you have thus far been absorbing the conversation in silence. He recognizes a canny old hand when he sees one, and he believes he knows what you are thinking. There are serious technical challenges, not least that the aquifer below the city is plummeting and becoming more contaminated every year, poisonous chemicals and biological toxins seeping into it like adulterants into a heroin junkie's collapsing vein. Powerful water extraction and purification equipment will be needed, plus, in all likelihood, a plan to draw water from canals intended for agricultural use, fiercely contested water itself laden with pesticide and fertilizer runoff.

Yet he suspects it is not these obstacles giving you pause. No, the brigadier thinks, you are wary because you know full well that when we military-related businesses advance into a market, the front lines change rapidly. We get permissions no one else can get. Red tape dissolves effortlessly for us. And reappears around our competitors. So we can move fast. Which makes us dangerous commercial adversaries. But it also makes our projects more exciting. And in this case we are going ahead whether you partner with us or not. Better, surely, to be close to us than to be yet another incumbent we swat aside. Besides, at least in the near term, we are simply offering too much cash for you to walk away.

"Yes," you say inevitably, and as expected.

The brigadier nods. "Very good. We'll have the RFP delivered to you by the start of next week. Gentlemen."

He rises and the meeting comes to an end.

That evening one of your four pump-action-shotgun-wielding uniformed security guards leaves the kiosk abutting your steel gate for a patrol along the perimeter of your property. In two twelve-hour shifts of two, along with barbed-wire-topped boundary walls and a personal nine-millimeter automatic in your locked desk drawer, guards are a key component of the measures you have taken to defend your mansion against would-be robbers, kidnappers, and underhanded business rivals, the constant threats your wealth engenders. This guard, a retired infantryman, subsists on a combination of his wages from a protection-services firm, his holiday bonuses from you, and his military pension. In exchange for the last, or perhaps out of a less transactional patriotism, his eyes and ears remain at the disposal of national security, making him a tiny part of those vast hives of clandestine human assets abuzz not just in your city but in all cities and in all countries, throughout the world.

At this moment his eyes and ears, or his eyes, rather, the

distance rendering his ears of somewhat diminished utility, would allow him to report that you are visible through a window, seated at the dining table of your wing of the house, awaiting, as is usual at this hour, the arrival of your son, who can be seen traversing the foyer that separates your wing from that of your wife. She is a lady well regarded for the charitable religious nonprofit she runs, and when the guard is working the day shift, by far his most frequent tasks are receiving the registered envelopes that stream to her with donations and opening and shutting the gate for her spirited band of piously attired female volunteers.

It is common knowledge among your guards and other household employees that the split between you and your wife extends beyond the floor plan of your house, encompassing domains sexual and financial as well. Your wife invariably sleeps alone, and insists on paying her bills herself, which she does out of the modest salary she draws from her nonprofit. She has been overheard by her cleaning girl saying that she will cohabit with you only until your child reaches adulthood, a situation now just a couple of years off, and for the guard, who is aware of this plan, she cuts a devastatingly romantic figure, chaste and determined, the sight of her undyed graying hair, a lock of which occasionally slips into view, reliably bringing his senescent heart to a canter.

The guard watches you embrace your son as the boy arrives for dinner. Your son is tall for his age, already almost as tall as you are, but slender and effeminate, an agonizingly antisocial teenager who spends inordinate amounts of time self-exiled in his room. Yet you gaze upon him as though he were a champion, strong of body and keen of mind, a born leader of men. In the one hour each day that you dine with your son, it is said often in the household, you smile and laugh more than in the other twenty-three.

Through a crack in the curtains of your study, later that night, the guard sees you turn on a lamp and settle out of sight, alone. Your bearer enters with a tray containing your cholesterol and blood-thinning medications, a tablespoon of psyllium husk, and a glass of water. He leaves empty-handed. The light remains on, but from the guard's vantage point there are no further signs of your activity.

Online, however, you can be tracked, and indeed you are tracked, as are we all, as you proceed through your e-mails, catch up on the news, perform a search, and wind up lingering, incongruously, on the website of a furnishings boutique. There is little there, the site not offering ordering facilities or even a catalog. It merely has a home page with a few photos and text, a contact section with phone numbers, address, and a map, and a brief biography of the owner, a

woman in her sixties, judging from her picture, with an un-
orthodox and varied career. All in all, an odd spot in the
ether to capture the attention of a water industrialist. A log
of your internet wanderings indicates you have not visited it
before. Nor, subsequently, are you recorded visiting it again.

The website in question is registered in another city, to
the residential address of its owner, who like many, perhaps most, computer users has never concerned herself
overmuch with such matters as firewalls, system updates,
or anti-malware utilities. Accordingly, her laptop, sleek
and high-end machine though it is, is simply teeming with
digital fauna, much in the same manner as its keyboard is
teeming with unseen bacteria and microorganisms, except
that among its uninvited coded squatters is a military program that allows the machine's built-in camera and microphone to be activated and monitored remotely, something
no single-celled protozoan could likely pull off, transforming the laptop, in effect, into a covert surveillance device or,
depending on the intent of the administrator of its monitor-
ing software, into an originator of voyeuristic striptease
and porn.

Currently, however, nothing so titillating seems to be in
the offing. The computer sits open on a counter, and through
its camera a woman can be seen by herself at a low table,

finishing off a meal and a bottle of red wine. The pretty girl
sits attentively, not looking at her hands or her food, but
music is audible, and then conversation, and then a rain-
storm, until it becomes obvious that she is watching a film.
When it is over she turns off the lights and disappears from
view. A running faucet can vaguely be heard. She emerges
into her bedroom, visible through its open doorway, wearing pajamas and cleansing her face with a series of round
cotton pads and liquid from a transparent vial. She shuts
her bedroom door, locking it, the sound of a sliding bolt
registering on her laptop's microphone. A lamp is extinguished and the glow seeping out around her door frame
comes to an end.

The following night the pretty girl arrives home late,
dressed as though she has attended a party, in a high-necked,
sleeveless top baring arms supple and veiny and strong. But
the night after that the pretty girl is again alone, consuming
a solitary meal with wine while watching a film, and on this
third night she receives a phone call. The caller is a woman,
easily identified as the pretty girl's assistant, for the mobile
she uses is linked to an e-mail account with messages chron-
icling her activities for the pretty girl's boutique.

A recording of their conversation reveals a tone of
warmth, these two clearly being not just colleagues but

friends. They discuss a purchasing trip to a tropical country famed for its lush forests, its numerous islands, and its volcanic mountains, as well as, presumably, its furniture. From her laptop's camera the pretty girl appears animated, excited, these trips abroad seeming to be something she looks forward to. Her assistant informs her that their visas have arrived, their flights and hotels are booked, and their local contacts are notified and ready. The names of restaurants are mentioned, and of a type of music they intend to see performed. Departure is only a week away.

The pretty girl smiles after their chat. Her laptop is angled away from her bedroom, so this evening her pre-sleep rituals cannot be seen. What can be seen are the steel bars on her windows, heavy in gauge and narrowly spaced, and a square motion sensor mounted high on her wall. Beneath it, near her front door, is a keypad belonging to her home alarm system. A light on the control panel goes from green to red, signaling that it is now armed. Perhaps this happens automatically, at a preprogrammed time. Or perhaps the pretty girl has activated it from a sister unit kept close at hand.

On the streets outside, a phone call reporting gunfire is being made to a police station. No one is immediately dispatched to investigate. Elsewhere a headless body missing the fingers of both hands will be recovered from a beach.

Crime statistics will confirm that a significant number of prosperous residents are presently in the process of being burgled or robbed. Contact between extremes of wealth and poverty fuels such incidents, of course. But the organized underworld's battles for turf overshadow any individual attempts at the armed redistribution of jewelry or mobile phones, and so, even in this most unequal city, the vast majority of tonight's violence will be inflicted upon neighborhoods whose residents are reliably poor.

Paramilitary forces are deployed to prevent such battles from spilling over too easily into areas deemed vital to national security, the port, for example, or upscale housing enclaves, or those premier commercial avenues from which rise headquarters of major corporations and banks. Indeed a paramilitary checkpoint is, at this moment, in operation a stone's throw from the towering headquarters of the bank that holds the accounts of the pretty girl, her boutique, and her assistant.

An examination of its records reveals that the pretty girl, while not swimming in cash, has a decent buffer set aside for a rainy day, and that the revenues of her boutique fluctuate but manage on average to stay ahead of expenses. Her assistant has a capped signing authority on the boutique's account, indicative of a rare level of trust, and a respectable salary that has been raised steadily over the course of the decade and a half she has been in the pretty girl's employ. Her assistant's monthly payments of home utilities, and of rent, coupled with a complete absence of expenditure on children's schooling, suggests she too may live alone, or perhaps with elderly parents, for her credit card also shows frequent medical costs, charges from a variety of doctors and diagnostic centers and hospitals, charges at times exceeding her wages, yet on a regular basis paid off in full by the pretty girl, with a direct transfer of the required amount from her personal account to that of her assistant.

Atop the bank's skyscraping offices are blinking lights meant to ward off passing aircraft, lights that glow serenely, high above the city. Below, as seen through helipad security cameras, parts of the metropolis are in darkness, electricity shortages meaning that the illumination of entire areas is turned off on a rotating basis, usually but not always on the hour, and in these inky patches, at this late time, little can be seen, just the odd building with its own generator, the bright headlamp-lit artery of a main road, or, on a winding side street, so faint as possibly to be imagined, the red-tracer swerve of a lone motorcycle seeking to avoid some danger unknown.

A week later the city is a sun-drenched maze of beiges and dirty creams receding beneath a jetliner on which the pretty girl and her assistant are registered passengers as it climbs into the sky and heads out to sea. It is picked up by the radar of a warship in international waters, identified as a commercial flight posing no immediate threat, and then for the most part ignored, the naval vessel using its antennae to continue to sniff the pheromone-like emissions of electrons wafting from coastal military installations instead.

The jetliner rises through a bank of scattered clouds. At roughly the same altitude, albeit far inland, an experimental unmanned aerial vehicle cruises in the opposite direction. It is small and limited in range. Its chief advantages are its low cost, allowing it to be procured in large numbers, and its comparative quietness, permitting it to function unobtrusively. There are high hopes for its success in the export market, in particular among police forces and cash-strapped armies engaged in urban operations.

On the outskirts of the city over which this drone is today validating its performance parameters, a crowd is gathering at a graveyard. Two vehicles stand out among those parked nearby. One is a van, emblazoned with the name and phone number of a commercial spray painter, possibly even belonging to the deceased, for it is being used as a hearse to transport his white-shrouded body. The other is a luxury automobile from which emerges a pair of male figures in suits, a man in his sixties and a slender, teenage boy, perhaps his grandson. These two are conspicuously well dressed, contrasting with most of the other mourners, yet they must be closely related to the fellow who has died, since they lend their shoulders to the task of bearing his corpse to the fresh-dug pit. The elder of them now commences to sob, his torso flexing spasmodically, as though wracked by a series of coughs. He looks up to the heavens.

The drone circles a few times, its high-powered eye unblinking, and flies observantly on.

TEN

DANCE WITH DEBT

WE MUST HURRY. WE ARE NEARING OUR END, YOU and I, and this self-help book too, well, the self in it anyway, and likewise the help it offers, though its bookness, being bookness, may by definition yet persevere.

As my writer's fingers key and your reader's eyes flick, you stand at the cusp of the eighth decade of your life, substantially bald, mostly thin, resolutely erect. Your parents have died, your surviving sister and brother survive no longer, your wife has left you and married a man closer to herself in outlook and in age, and your son has chosen not to return after studying in North America, which, despite Asia's rise, retains some attraction for a young conceptual artist with craggy hip bones and lips like buttered honey.

Through the window of your office you see your city

mutating around you, its zoning and planning restrictions slipping away, deep foundation pits and skeletal building sites occupying land that only a few years ago aerial photography would have shown puffed over with opulent, pastry-esque villas. The sun is low and fat in your line of sight. A voice can be heard. It emanates from your former brother-in-law, still your deputy, sitting behind you and once again entreating you to take on more debt.

In this he is surely right. With borrowed funds, a business can invest, gain leverage, and leverage is a pair of wings. Leverage is flight. Leverage is a way for small to be big and big to be huge, a glorious abstraction, the promise of tomorrow today, yes, a liberation from time, the resounding triumph of human will over dreary, chronology-shackled physical reality. To leverage is to be immortal.

Or if not, your deputy asserts, at least the converse is true.

"If we don't borrow," he says, "we'll die."

You turn from the window and reseat yourself opposite him. "You're getting carried away."

"We don't have scale. The sector's consolidating. In two years, there won't be a dozen water firms operating in this city. There'll be three. At most four. And we won't be one of them."

"We'll compete on quality."

"It's fucking water. We just provide to spec."

Increasingly, your deputy has begun speaking to you in tones that veer almost to the aggressive. Whether this is because he blames you for the collapse of your marriage to his sister, or because he, a younger man, fears you less and less as age exacts its toll on your body, or because he is at last confident of his own indispensability to the smooth running of your operation, you do not know.

"That's not true," you say.

"It's true enough. Either we buy a competitor or we sell. Or we'll rot away."

"We're not putting ourselves up for sale."

"That's what you always say. So let's buy."

"We've never taken on that much debt."

"It's risky. A gamble. But one we'll have a good chance of winning."

You catch at that moment a reflection of your ex-wife in the form of your deputy, glimpsing, as you do periodically, a telltale flourish of the genetic hand that drew both their lines, beautiful in her case, rather comedic in his. You trust him. Not entirely, but enough. And more than that, you sense he may have a better understanding of the future course of your business than you do. But most of all, you no longer

care so passionately about the outcome. Of late, you have
had the impression of merely going through the motions of
your life, of rising, shaving, bathing, dressing, coming in to
work, attending meetings, taking phone calls, returning
home, eating, shitting, lying in bed, all out of habit, for no
real purpose, like the functioning of some legacy water
meter, cut off from the billing system, whose measurements
swirl by unrecorded.

And so you say, "All right. Let's do it."

Your deputy is pleased. For his part, he regards himself
as a mostly loyal member of your team. Mostly loyal because he has secretly skimmed only enough funds from
your firm over the past two decades to cause no real harm,
money he has squirreled abroad, far out of sight, as a measure of insurance should his employment come suddenly to
an end. But testing times lie ahead, the viability of your enterprise is itself at stake, and despite being well paid, your
deputy has saved too little, living the lifestyle of an owner
rather than a manager, and now may be his last chance to
capture a more meaningful slice of the pie. Buying another
company offers him the prospect of pocketing a sizable
kickback, an unofficial golden parachute he considers very
much his due.

That evening you ride home alone, in the rear of your
limousine, behind your uniformed chauffeur and a guard

who clutches an assault rifle upright against his torso. At each traffic light people attach themselves to your window in supplication, beggars, one armless, one toothless, one a hermaphrodite with white-powdered face and down-slanting smile. You see a man on a motorcycle bearing also his wife and children turn off his engine as he waits for the signal to change. Through fourteen speakers and four sub-woofers your radio purrs a report of a series of bomb blasts in a crowded market on the coast. You curse resignedly. If riots flare in protest, a consignment of yours could be stuck in port.

Over the coming months your business is quantified, digitized, and jacked into a global network of finance, your activities subsumed with barely a ripple in a collective mathematical pool of ever-changing current and future cash flows. A syndicate of banks is rallied, covenants sworn to, offices and trucks and equipment and even your personal residence pledged as collateral, an acquisition war chest electronically credited with booty, a target hailed, and the basic terms of its capitulation negotiated. The proposed deal is high priced but not exorbitant, with a plausible opportunity for success.

Thus the matter might have rested had fate, or narrative trajectory, in the form of coronary artery disease, not taken a hand. You are attempting to sleep when the pain begins, mild, a numbness proceeding down one arm. You turn on a lamp and sit up. It is then that an invisible girder slams into your chest, surely flattening it, forcing you to shut your eyes. You cannot breathe. The pressure is unbearable. But it recedes, and you are left weak and vaguely nauseated, your scrawny limbs sweating inside your thin cotton pajamas despite the chill. You open your eyes. Your thorax is intact. You unfasten a button and run your fingers along your ribs, your nails too long and slightly dirty, your hair there white and coiled. No wound can be seen, but the man you touch feels brittle. In the morning, still awake, you go to see your doctor.

The hospital is large and crowded, charitable donations, including from you, ensuring many of the patients it admits are desperately poor. A village woman on the verge of death lies on a bench, her look of bafflement reminding you of your mother. You are unable to walk unaided and so you lean on your chauffeur. You stumble, and embarrassingly he lifts you off the ground, easily, as he might a child or a youthful bride. You order him to put you in a wheelchair. Your voice is hoarse, and you have to repeat yourself. A man dabs with a filthy mop at what appears to be a trail of urine, telling people mostly ineffectually not to step in it.

Your doctor has come out of his examination room to greet you, an unprecedented honor. He smiles in his usual manner, but forgoes his customary wagging of the finger as though you have been naughty, and instead says in a cheerful tone, "We'll be going straight to the intensive-care unit." He wheels you inside himself, telling your chauffeur he is not permitted to follow but should certainly remain in the hall, as he may be needed.

You are fortunate that your second heart attack takes place in the ICU. When you regain consciousness, you have become a kind of cyborg, part man, part machine. Electrodes connect your chest to a beeping computer terminal mounted on a rack, and a pair of transparent tubes channel oxygen from a nearby metal tank to your nostrils and fluids from a plastic pouch into your bloodstream through a needle taped at your wrist. You panic and start to flail, but your limbs barely move and you are gently restrained. A nurse speaks. You have difficulty following her words. You understand, though, that for the moment this apparatus and you are inseparable.

To be a man whose life requires being plugged into machines, multiple machines, in your case interfaces electrical, gaseous, and liquid, is to experience the shock of an unseen network suddenly made physical, as a fly experiences a cobweb. The inanimate strands that cling to your precariously still-animate form themselves connect to other strands, to the hospital's power system, its backup generator, its information technology infrastructure, the unit that produces oxygen, the people who refill and circulate the tanks, the department that replenishes medications, the trucks that deliver them, the factories at which they are manufactured, the mines where requisite raw materials emerge, and on and on, from your body, into your room, across the building, and out the doors to the world beyond, mirroring in stark exterior reality preexisting and mercifully unconsidered systems within, the veins and nerves and sinews and lymph nodes without which there is no you. It is good you sleep.

When you next wake, your nephews are here, your brother's sons, and also, surprisingly, your ex-wife, along with her new husband, a bearded man with a fatherly demeanor that disorients you because he is practically a generation your junior. The illumination of your room is odd, futuristic, the artifact of either some advanced bulb technology or your addled mental state. Your doctor pats your hand and summarizes for you, in everyone's presence, your overall position and course of treatment. Your prognosis is less than peachy. The muscles of your heart have been damaged and the fraction of blood it is pumping per beat is dangerously low. Such a condition need not be immediately fatal, your doctor has himself had a patient who improved and lived on for years after a similar level of impairment. But you also have extensive blockages of the coronary arteries and so you face the imminent likelihood of a further heart attack, which would almost certainly be terminal. Yet in your situation a bypass or angioplasty is out of the question, and leaving the hospital, in your doctor's judgment, would also be unwise. It would be best to wait and see.

You understand this advice as a coded instruction to prepare to die, a thought reinforced by the wet film you observe dancing in the eyes of your ex-wife. She returns to the hospital each day, usually minus her husband. She is formal with you but also efficient, as though playing the role of a dedicated administrator in a movie. Under her supervision, second and third opinions are sought, a new cardiologist identified, and you moved to a different institution. A renowned world expert has agreed to see you in a few weeks, when he is next in your city, and it is on him that your ex-wife appears to pin her hopes.

This world expert is like a man from another planet, with an orange glow to his skin, unnaturally white teeth, and hair so thick he could safely ride a motorcycle without a helmet. Upon examining you and considering your file, he says there is no reason that a few stents in your arteries should not do the trick. There is, of course, a modest chance of dying on the operating table, but since there is a very good chance of dying soon off of it, the risk seems outweighed by the potential reward.

You agree to the procedure. It is performed while you are awake, disconcertedly watching on a monitor the camera feed from a robotic probe inside your body as tiny mechanical contraptions unspool and expand within you, forcing the flabby walls of your arteries open and locking them in place. You wonder whether, should anything go wrong, you will see your death depicted in the micro-battlefield on-screen before your brain ceases to function, or whether the internal chain of events will outpace the external relay, leaving you with simple blackness, despite everything this spaceship of an operating theater has to offer. The question remains theoretical, however, for the world expert declares your surgery an unmitigated success.

The following day, after your post-op checkup, he tells you that if, now resupplied with blood, your heart recovers as much as, despite your advanced age, he thinks it might, you are looking at many months, or even a few years, of un-hospitalized life. You thank him. You also thank your ex-wife. It is in this moment, glancing at the world expert and receiving a solemn, orange-hued nod, and asking you to relax and try to take the news without allowing yourself to get too agitated, she informs you that her brother, whom she now wishes had never been born, has absconded abroad with the funds your company raised for its planned acquisition, unable perhaps to resist the opportunity presented by your absence, and further that your company is consequently bankrupt, as are you, and that the policemen stationed outside your room are not there for your protection, as you have heretofore assumed, but rather because you are technically under arrest.

You take this news as well as possible, which is to say you do not die. You tell your ex-wife you have no doubt she had nothing to do with it, the error in hiring and trusting her brother being entirely yours, and you point out that, health-wise, you are feeling much better than you have in weeks. You do not mention that the earth's gravity and atmospheric pressure seem to have increased since your heart attacks, or that walking unassisted to the bathroom this morning was like circumnavigating the surface of an alien and inhospitable moon.

When she leaves, you sit in silence for an entire day. Then you get to work. Your nephews access pockets of funds you have secreted away, which, because hidden, your creditors have not seized, and so you are able to hire a criminal lawyer, pay the necessary bribes, secure bail, and rent a room in a two-star hotel, all without needing to burden further your less-than-wealthy ex-wife. She refuses, though, while hanging her handsome, covered head, to allow you to reimburse her for the sizable costs of your medical treatment. It was the least she could do, she says.

As you now lack a driver or a car of your own, your nephews drive you to the hotel, railing against your deputy, whom they suspected was rotten ever since he eased them out of your firm years ago, adding quickly that they harbor no ill will towards you, you are their uncle, and blood is stronger than such disappointments. They ask you to move in with them. You express gratitude but say you are more used to being alone. Through the windscreen you see dust and pollution suspended over the city like a dome, transforming the sky to copper and the clouds to irradiated bronze.

In the months that follow, you receive anonymous death threats and meet with politicians you thought were allies but prove barely able to conceal their gloating. You are caught up in one of the cynical accountability campaigns periodically launched by your city's establishment, tossed to the wolf pack of public opinion, unsubstantiated rumors of your shady dealings receiving scandalized attention in newspapers. You have always been an outsider, and finally you have been wounded. It is only natural that you be sacrificed so that the rest of the herd may prance on.

Once this outcome is clear, you accept your fate without

too much resistance, struggling, to the extent you do, largely out of habit and a sense of responsibility for your ex-employees. It almost seems that a part of you perversely welcomes being humbled in this way, that you suffer from some mad impulse to slough off your wealth, like an animal molting in the autumn. Perhaps this contributes to the frenzy with which you are attacked. When it is over, your financial bones retain only tiny slivers of their former meat, but you have not been picked entirely clean. You are not destitute. You remain unincarcerated. You are an old man in a hotel room, taking your medication, looking out the dirty window at the street below, traveling by taxi when you must.

In person you sometimes appear timid, hesitant, though whether this change is due to your economic misfortune or the decline in your health, it is impossible to say. You have encountered the reality that with age things are snatched from a man, often suddenly and without warning. You do not rent a home for yourself or buy a secondhand car. Instead you remain in your hotel, with few possessions, no more than might fit in a single piece of luggage. This suits you. Having less means having less to anesthetize you to your life.

Near the hotel is an internet cafe. You walk there now, slowly. Because you are easily winded and must pause to rest, you carry the ultra-light shaft of plastic and metal your doctor refers to, perhaps nostalgically, as a cane. You have spent more time on this earth than have all three of the young technicians who work in the cafe combined. Their T-shirts and tattoos and stylized whiskers are symbols of a clan with which you are unfamiliar. They are not pleased to see you. But their leader, a youth with a notch razored into his brow, at least rises with a semblance of respect.

"If you wouldn't mind helping me again," you say.

He nods. "Number five."

His manner is brusque, but he is thorough as he ensures you are set up and ready to proceed. You are seated in a cubicle, on a chair of firm yet comfortable mesh. In front of you is a flat monitor with a readout of time utilized and money owed. Invisible below the surface of your desk, but touchable with your feet, is a shin-tall computer from which you carefully pivot away lest you do some harm. Though small, these cubicles have partitions higher than those in your late firm's offices, designed to afford users a maximum of privacy. The cafe is dark, with no active source of illumination other than its screens, and smells vaguely of women's hair spray, sweat, and semen.

Your son materializes before you at an angle suggesting you are looking down at him from above. You sit straighter, unconsciously trying to raise your head to a height from which this perspective would be normal, but it has no effect on your sense of slight disorientation. You do not know what to do with your hands, so you grip the armrests of your chair. Your son freezes, pixelates, and then, flowing again, speaks.

"Dad."

"My boy."

He is in his apartment, a warehouse of a room sparsely furnished with reappropriated building materials, his dining table two stacks of cinder blocks supporting a horizontal door with hinges intact. Outside his windows it is night. He inquires concernedly after your health, you reassure him that all is well, and you chat about politics, the economy, his cousins. He has been unable to visit you because his visa status is linked to a long-standing asylum petition. A trip home would undermine his claim that he is in danger.

"Have you spoken to your mother?" you ask.

"No. Not in a while."

"You should. She misses you."

"I'm sure she does, in her way."

Your son's friend passes behind him, shirtless, unshaven, sleepy. The friend is brushing his teeth, preparing for bed. He waves to you and you lift a palm in reply. Your son smiles, half turns to his friend, voices something inaudible, and redirects himself to the camera of his computer.

"It's getting late," he says apologetically.

"Yes, don't let me keep you."

"When's your next doctor's visit?"

"Today."

"Promise to text me how it goes."

You say you will. The sticky headphones on your ears emit an aquatic plop and your son's image disappears as though it has been sucked down a hole the size of a single pixel in the center of your screen. Where before there were brightness and movement there is now only stillness, save for the time and money counters ticking along in a corner. You settle your bill and pass on.

At this moment the pretty girl is also scrutinizing a computer, reviewing with her assistant the month's sales figures, which make for somber reading. Tonight she too will journey to a hospital, though of course presently she does not know it.

"It's shaping into quite a drop," she says. She smiles tightly. "I hope you're ready for the bounce."

"More than ready," her assistant says.

She considers. "Doesn't look like we have a choice."

"No."

"Fine. Cancel the spring procurement trip."

The two of them are silent.

"There's always the fall," her assistant says.

The pretty girl nods. "Yes. There's always that."

She leaves her furniture boutique at her customary hour, five o'clock, her driver making haste to beat the traffic, though his efforts must contest with dug-up roads. The pretty girl peers out her window at recurring series of slender pits. Cabling is going in, seemingly everywhere, mysterious cabling, black- or gray- or orange-clad, snaking endlessly off spools into the warm, sandy soil. She wonders what on earth it binds together.

It is her assistant's job to close the boutique, later that evening, and her assistant has done so, and is supervising the manager's counting of the day's take, in preparation for placing it overnight in the safe, when a brick is thrown beneath half-lowered steel shutters to smash the glass shop door. The pretty girl's assistant hears this in a small office out back and sees, in crisp monochrome, on a CCTV display, three armed men enter, their faces partially concealed. Instinctively, she activates a silent alarm, locks the money away, and spins the combination wheel, all to the horror of the manager, who now fears getting out of this situation alive.

The armed men appear to know an alarm has been triggered, and perhaps as a result their leader makes as if to shoot the manager through the forehead without a word.

But he thinks better of it and tells the pretty girl's assistant to open the safe. When, out of confusion rather than bravery, she hesitates, he hits her on the temple with the butt of his rifle, not too forcefully, given her age and gender, but firmly enough to knock her to the floor. She rises and complies. The armed men pocket the money. In total, the robbery lasts no longer than five minutes. Private guards arrive in nine, the pretty girl in twenty-two, and the police in thirty-eight.

As a precaution, due to the blow her assistant has received, the pretty girl brings her to an emergency room. She puts her hand on her assistant's in the car, holds her fingers gently, the less elderly woman stunned and staring straight ahead, mostly unspeaking. A harried nurse glances at the pretty girl's assistant, says it is a bruise, nothing more, suggests an ice pack and some analgesics, and sends them on their way. During the drive home, her assistant complains of dizziness and nausea. The pretty girl takes her back to the hospital, her assistant convulses and loses consciousness in transit, and when a doctor pries open her eyelids and shines a torch at her pupils she is already past revival and soon dead.

It is on this evening that the pretty girl's forty-year affair with her adopted metropolis comes to an end, though she does not leave right away. Time passes as her decision gathers within her. She must also sell her shop and conclude certain practical matters. But something has changed, and her direction is not in doubt. She will sit alone in her living room, gazing out through bars at the night, at the lights of aircraft ascending in the sky, and feel a tug, of what she cannot say, no, not exactly, only that it pulls her with soft finality, and that it emanates from the city of her birth.

ELEVEN

FOCUS ON THE FUNDAMENTALS

I SUPPOSE I SHOULD CONSIDER AT THIS STAGE CON-
fessing to certain false pretenses, to certain subterfuges
that may have been perpetrated here, certain of-hands that
may have been, um, sleighted. But I won't. Not just yet.
Though filthy richness is admittedly gone from your grasp,
this book is going to maintain a little longer its innocence,
or at least the non-justiciability of its guilt, and continue
offering, through economic advice, help to two selves, one of
them yours, the other mine.

As luck would have it, this advice is unaffected by the
loss of your wealth, since it applies to those of modest means
too. And the advice is this. Focus on the fundamentals. Blow
through the fluff, see the forest for the trees, prioritize

what's core to your operation. Right now, in your case, that means cutting costs to the bone.

You have done so admirably well. At the two-star hotel that is your residence, you have negotiated a long-term, month-by-month room rental for less than half the standard rate, taking full advantage of both your willingness to pay cash and the fact that you once gave a job to the hotel manager's late father, who described you with undying, referring of course to the sentiment, not the man, veneration. You also eat sparingly, your metabolism having slowed enough for you to make do with a single meal a day, you scrimp on transportation by using taxis instead of bearing the expense of owning and operating a car, and you avoid being saddled with hefty phone bills by conducting your weekly conversations with your son from an internet cafe. Thus the majority of your limited savings remains untouched, available for doctor's visits, tests, and medications, and it seems not improbable that in the race between death and destitution, you can look forward to the former emerging victorious.

Your one indulgence is the serving of tea and biscuits you provide to your supplicants, without fail, in the cramped lobby of your hotel. The building itself is perhaps ten years in age, though it could equally easily be thirty, pressed between two other structures of similarly four-storied height, malnourished width, and indeterminate date of construction, on what was formerly an access road to a quiet market but now lies within the ever-expanding boundaries of a bustling and amorphously amoeba-shaped zone of commerce. Nearby, animals are slaughtered, pastries baked, high-fidelity speaker crossovers tweaked, fake imported cigarettes distributed, and blast-resistant window film retailed, the last with promises of free installation, a not insignificant plus, given that precise and labor-intensive squeegeeing is needed to expel unsightly air bubbles.

The clansmen who come to you are often, but not always, recently arrived from their villages, unskilled or semi-skilled hands in search of jobs in construction or transport or domestic service, and so they look around at the worn common areas of your hotel with awe, taking the mechanical door and steel buttons of its non-functional elevator and the daintiness of its teacups and saucers as confirmation that you are, as they have been told, an important man, an impression further reinforced by the fine tailoring of your clothes and the distinguished bearing that you, despite your age and setbacks, have mostly managed to retain. You help them as best you can, making calls, putting in a good word, and answering in painstaking detail their many questions.

But not all of your supplicants are rural youngsters. Some are city boys, first generation, as you once were, or second, with jaunty haircuts and savvy, quick-moving faces. Others are older, professionals, managers even, on occasion dressed in suit and tie. For these more urbane callers your abode is something of a disappointment, but their misgivings usually abate in conversation, when it becomes clear you are a man who speaks knowledgeably, and a generous listener too, albeit one slightly hard of hearing. They are eager to mine your network of business and government contacts, a diminishing vein you are nonetheless content to prospect on their behalf, and it is not altogether infrequent that you turn up a nugget of assistance.

You accept no financial reward for your contributions, no placement fees or referral tokens, nor do you hunger after the expressions of gratitude bestowed upon you. Your motivations stem from different sources, from lingering desires to connect and to be of use, from the need to fill a few of the long hours of the week, and from curiosity about the world beyond, about the comings and goings and toings and froings of that great city outside your hotel, in which you have passed almost the entirety of your life, and of which you once knew so much.

You hear reports that the water table continues to drop,

the thirst of many millions driving bore after steel bore deeper and deeper into the aquifer, to fill countless leaky pipes and seepy, unlined channels, phenomena with which you are intimately familiar and from which you have profited, but which are now contributing in places to a noticeable desiccation of the soil, to a transformation of moist, fertile, hybrid mud into cracked, parched, pure land. Meanwhile similar attempts, both official and non, seem to be under way to try to desiccate society itself, through among other things creeping restrictions on festivals and the public pursuit of fun, with a similar result, cracks, those widening fissures evident between young people, who appear to you divided as never before, split into myriad, incomprehensible tribes, signaling their affiliations with an automobile sticker, a bare shoulder, or some arcane permutation in the possibilities for facial hair.

You often do not know, when you venture forth into the streets on your errands, who among them stands for what. Nor is it at all clear to you that they themselves, beneath the poses they strike, really know what they stand for either, any more than you did at their age. But what you do sense, what is unmistakable, is a rising tide of frustration and anger and violence, born partly of the greater familiarity the poor today have with the rich, their faces pressed to that clear window on wealth afforded by ubiquitous television, and partly of the change in mentality that results from an outward shift in the supply curve for firearms. At times, watching the stares that follow a luxury SUV as it muscles its way down a narrow road, you are nearly relieved to have been already separated from your fortune.

If, while I write, I can't be certain that you have had no inkling of your proximity to the pretty girl, still it stands to reason that this should be true. She resides about thirty minutes from your hotel as the crow flies, but since the urban crow tends to fly circuitously, and with many pauses, she may not be that far, or she may be much farther. She owns a small townhouse, of which she is landlady, renting her two spare rooms at below-market rates to a pair of women, one a singer, the other an actress, early in their careers and neither quite yet a success. Between her savings and this rental income, the pretty girl gets by.

Perhaps because of a persistent twinge in her hip, she ventures out less than she formerly did. She leaves most household chores to her factotum, a diminutive, middle-aged man who cooks, drives, shops, and occupies a servant quarter next to her kitchen. She does however make a daily round of her favorite park, walking slowly but erectly, in the evenings during summer and fall, and in the mornings during winter and spring, when she particularly enjoys observing the youthful lovers who gather there for hurried, furtive liaisons before they report to class or to work.

At home she watches movies and, especially, listens to the radio, often turning the volume high enough that it amuses her tenants, who might take a break from their busy lives to chat with her for a few moments as she nods her head to the beat and puffs along on her cigarette. Sometimes one of them will share with her their latest work, a video clip or demo of a song, but this is rare. She is never invited to a set or a studio. Her townhouse is at the end of a cul-de-sac, and from her upstairs lounge she can see all the way down her street, past a stretch of shops and restaurants, to a telecommunications center from which red and white masts soar mightily, towering above satellite dishes, like electromagnetic spars built to navigate the clouds. She bought her place for its view.

Hers is not by nature a temperament sympathetic to nostalgia, in fact the opposite. She refuses to visit the seaside metropolis where she spent so many productive years. Nor does she seek to scrape together the funds to retain, on a temporary basis, a new assistant who could translate and facilitate for her, making possible a final coda to her much-loved trips abroad. In her mind, her return to the region of her birth marked a decisive break from days gone recently by.

And yet, whether because of her advancing age or the strange echoes this city sustains through its associations with her childhood, she finds herself pulled into frequent and unexpected turns of thought, dampness on a fingertip used to wipe dew off a glass of water reminding her of a gentle and now-dead photographer, say, or a sudden breeze felt on her balcony conjuring up a beach party long ago. Present and alert in this moment, she, unaccustomedly, might well be lost to reverie in the next.

You reencounter each other at a pharmacy, a crowded micro-warehouse stacked with pallets not much bigger than matchboxes, mostly white, bearing text too minute to be legible, even while squinting, and, on occasion, iridescent seals of hologrammed authenticity that shimmer like fish in the light. You are progressing incrementally to the counter, buffeted by those who push forward out of line, reliant on strangers who acknowledge you and are good enough to wait. Ahead you see a figure turn after paying for her purchase, a figure you think you recognize, and you are seized by a powerful emotion. This emotion is akin to panic, and indeed you consider shoving your prescription back into your pocket and making for the exit.

But you stand your ground. As the figure approaches, she frowns.

"Is that you?" she asks, not for the first time in her life.

You lean on your cane and scrutinize the wizened woman before you.

"Yes," you say.

Neither of you speaks. Slowly, she shakes her head. She rests her hand on yours, her skin smooth and cool against your knuckles.

"Do I look as old as you do?" she asks.

"No," you say.

"I thought you were an honest boy."

You smile. "Not always."

"Let's find a place to sit down."

Near the pharmacy is a coffee shop, evidently part of a chain, and possessed of a franchise's artificial quirkiness, its seemingly mismatched sofas and chairs and tables corresponding to a precise and determined scheme set forth in the experience section of a corporate brand guidelines binder. Its furniture and fittings evoke decades gone by. Its music, its menu, and, saliently, its prices are utterly contemporary. For affluent younger customers, the effect might be pleasant, transporting them from this street in this neighborhood to a virtual realm inhabited by people very much like themselves across rising Asia, or even across the planet. But for you, who remembers that a fruit seller occupied this

particular property until a few months ago, the faux worn-
ness of this establishment would be disorienting. Normally.
Today you do not notice.

Over tea you and the pretty girl discuss what ex-lovers
meeting again after half a lifetime usually discuss, namely
your health, the arcs of your careers, shared memories, yes,
this often while laughing, as well as your present whereabouts, and, in passing, so tangentially as merely to be
grazed, whether you are currently single. Your waiter is
courteous, seeing a pair of elderly people leaning forward,
engrossed in conversation, which is, of course, what you see
also, except that it is not all you see, for you see too, overlaid
on the pretty girl's diminished form, or perhaps rather flickering inside it, a taller, stronger, more zestful entity, happy
in this moment, and able yet to dance in the moistness of
an eye.

"How strange to be using the word retired," the pretty
girl says as she finishes her tea.

"We're unemployed," you correct her. "Sounds more
alive than retired."

"Are you looking for work?"

"No."

"Retired, then."

You pour two glasses of water.

"You should interview me," you say, passing her hers. "And I'll interview you. Then we'll be unemployed."

She takes a sip. "Only if neither of us gets hired."

You call her the next day, and in the weeks that follow you spend time together, going to a restaurant for dinner one evening, on another converging in a park for a slow-moving stroll. You explore the city's main colonial-era museum and its pungently aromatic zoo, attractions you last visited when your son was a schoolboy. At the zoo you are surprised by how inexpensive tickets are, and further by the size of the facility, which seems bigger than you recall, though you had expected the opposite to be the case. The pretty girl marvels at the aviary, you at hippopotamuses slipping daintily into a mud pool from the grassy banks of their enclosure. She draws to your attention the large number of young men who are here, their accents and dialects often hailing from remote districts. They call to the animals in amusement and wonder, or sit in clusters on plentiful benches, taking advantage of the shade. The zoo has signs listing the daily dietary intake of its most prominent residents, and occasionally a literate visitor is to be heard reading to his fellows the prodigious quantities of food required to maintain such and such beast.

In the pretty girl's company, you give up a small degree

of the physical isolation you had imposed upon yourself, venturing out into the city a little more, having, through the presence of a friend, greater reason to do so than you did before, and also, when part of a group of two people, being less afraid than when alone. Yes, the city remains intermittently perilous, in, for example, the slashing thrusts of its vehicles, the ferocious extremes of its temperatures, and the antibiotic resistance of its microorganisms, not to mention the forcefulness of its human predators, and particularly at your age you must stay on your guard. But you savor your tentative, shared reentry, and think that the city may not be quite so fearsome, that indeed, when gazed upon with the good humor that can come from companionship, significant swaths of it appear mostly navigable, at least for the present, while a measure of bodily vitality endures.

At times the pretty girl feels shocked looking at you, the shock of being mortal, of seeing you as a cane-propped mirror, of your frail and gaunt form's inescapable contemporaneity to her own. These impressions tend to occur in the first moments of your encounters, when an absence of a few days has run itself like a soft cloth over her short-term visual memory. But quickly other data begin to accrue, likely starting with your eyes and your mouth, her image of you resolving itself into something different, something timeless, or if not entirely timeless, still beautiful, handsome to behold. She sees in the cock of your head your awareness of the world around you, in your hands your armored gentleness, in your chin your temper. She sees you as a boy and as a man. She sees how you diminish her solitude, and, more meaningfully, she sees you seeing, which sparks in her that oddest of desires an I can have for a you, the desire that you be less lonely.

One night, after a movie in a theater that astonishes you with the size of its screen and the quality of its sound and the costliness of its popcorn, and also with the suddenness of the fight that breaks out among teenagers outside, in which you are knocked to the ground by mistake as a member of the crowd backs up, and you receive a bad bruise on your thigh, but nothing is broken, thank goodness, the pretty girl invites you over to her place. Her tenants grin as you enter, clearly delighted to see that their landlady has a gentleman caller, and with knowing glances make themselves scarce.

"Would you like a drink?" the pretty girl asks.

"I'm not supposed to," you say.

"A half glass of wine?"

You nod.

She retrieves an opened bottle from the refrigerator. "Sit, sit," she says, and pours for you both.

The two of you sip at your glasses. A silence descends.

"Should we just go to my room?" she asks.

"Yes."

She leads you by the hand and shuts the door behind you. She does not turn on the light.

"One second," she says, heading to her bathroom.

You worry about your balance in the darkness.

"Where's the bed?"

"Oh, sorry." She directs you with a palm at your waist. "Here."

You sit down. The mattress is firm. You grope with your hand and, finding a wall, carefully lean your cane against it. A faint light emerges from beneath the door of the bathroom, and sounds emanate from within, scraping, running water, the flush of a commode. You need to use a toilet yourself, but you suppress the impulse. The pretty girl is gone for a while.

When she returns she sits beside you. You kiss. She tastes of mouthwash. She has changed into a nightie and through its fabric your hand can feel her ribs, her belly, the unbelievable softness of her breast like a second set of skin. She helps you undress. She tugs at you rhythmically, and fortunately you become hard, perhaps benefitting from the pressure of your full bladder on your prostate. She applies between her legs an ointment from a jar on her bedside table, and lies on her side with her back to your chest. You fumble a bit but are able to enter her. You move. She touches herself. You hug her with one arm.

Neither of you reaches your finish. You begin to deflate before that moment comes. But, I should add, you do reach pleasure, and a measure of comfort, and lying there afterwards, temporarily thwarted and a little embarrassed, you unexpectedly start to chuckle, and she joins you, and it is the best and warmest laugh either of you has had in some time.

TWELVE

HAVE AN EXIT
STRATEGY

THIS BOOK, I MUST NOW CONCEDE, MAY NOT HAVE been the very best of guides to getting filthy rich in rising Asia. An apology is no doubt due. But at this late juncture, apologies alone can achieve little. Far more useful, I propose, to address ourselves to our inevitable exit strategies, yours and mine, preparation, in this lifelong case, being most of the battle.

We are all refugees from our childhoods. And so we turn, among other things, to stories. To write a story, to read a story, is to be a refugee from the state of refugees. Writers and readers seek a solution to the problem that time passes, that those who have gone are gone and those who will go, which is to say every one of us, will go. For there was a moment when anything was possible. And there will be a moment when nothing is possible. But in between we can create.

As you create this story and I create this story, I would like to ask you how things were. I would like to ask you about the person who held your hand when dust entered your eye or ran with you from the rain. I would like to tarry here awhile with you, or if tarrying is impossible, to transcend my here, with your permission, in your creation, so tantalizing to me, and so unknown. That I can't do this doesn't stop me from imagining it. And how strange that when I imagine, I feel. The capacity for empathy is a funny thing.

As an illustration, let us consider a fish unable to burp. We can see it now, suspended in its glass bowl, floating weightlessly in a cloud-puffed sky. Its water is so transparent as to be invisible, and were it not for its bowl, it would look as if it were flying in the air, perhaps propelled about by the fluttering of its little fins. It has escaped from the seas, from the lakes, from the ponds, and it dangles now, free, bathed in sunlight and in warmth. And yet it is deeply troubled. It has a pang, a bubble trapped in its fish esophagus. Though heavenly, angelic, still it suffers. It strains. And do our hearts go out to it? Yes, they do. Burp, dear friend. Why do you not burp?

Meanwhile, directly below this aerial ichthyological

drama, a mountain's height lower to be more precise, and therefore back on earth, an old man lives in a small town-house with an old woman. You and the pretty girl have moved in together. She has lost a tenant, and your mind has begun slightly to drift, not always, but on occasion you are unsure where you are, and for this reason residing in a hotel has become problematic. You do not share a bedroom, the pretty girl never having done so before and being of the view that it is a bit late to start, but you do share much of your days, by turns cheerfully, grumpily, quietly, or com-fortingly, and when the mood strikes you both, your nights, and you pool your dwindling savings, which are fast being eroded by inflation.

The two of you venture out less often, and the only other people you see with regularity are the pretty girl's one re-maining tenant, the actress, and the pretty girl's factotum, who assists you when you are disoriented, and who reminds you of your father, even though physically they are dissimi-lar. Maybe this is because he is an obedient man, and a house servant, and close to the age at which your father died.

Sitting on a reupholstered chair, a newspaper in your lap and loud music in your ear, to which the pretty girl nods her head as she smokes, and enjoying a temperate autumn afternoon, you are surprised to hear the bell ring and find yourself in the presence of your son. You had forgotten he was coming. You stand to greet him and are swept up in a ferocious yet protective hug. He kisses the pretty girl's cheek, and she too perceives time ripple as she sees a reflection of your younger self, albeit a better-dressed version with a mincing walk quite unlike your own. She offers him a cigarette, and to her satisfaction he accepts. You can sense she is taking a liking to the boy, which makes you happy. He has grown, though that must be unusual for a man of thirty, and even seated he towers above you.

It is the first visit in many years for your son, finally a citizen of his new country and free to travel, and you try to suppress your undercurrent of resentment at his decision to absent himself from your presence in so devastatingly severe a manner. You feel a love you know you will never be able to adequately explain or express to him, a love that flows one way, down the generations, not in reverse, and is understood and reciprocated only when time has made of a younger generation an older one. He tells you he has just been to meet your ex-wife. She is well, he says, and their reunion was tearful and affectionate, and he agreed not to speak of certain things and she for her part did not ask.

For a month you and the pretty girl are caught up in a whirlwind of engagements, mostly at home, your son cooking for you or bringing over a film, but twice outside also, at restaurants of his choosing, swanky places with newfangled decor, where he pays with his credit card. Then he is gone and your world shrinks to the townhouse once again. He has left you some cash, which is fortunate. A blast at a nearby bungalow, purportedly utilized to hold and interrogate suspects by an intelligence service in the past, shatters your windows, and you use the money to have them replaced.

The city beyond is an increasingly mythological space. It intrudes in the form of power and gas outages, traffic noises, and airborne particulates that cause you to wake wheezing in your bed. It can be glimpsed around curtains and through iron grilles. Television and radio also bring in some news of it, usually frightening, but then that has always been the case.

Frequently you have the impression of gazing with the pretty girl, as if from the lip of a cliff, off into a valley where night is falling, a stark and dry and contaminated valley, where perhaps all sorts of bony, mutating creatures abide, many of them carnivorous, and having had your share of carnivorous tendencies yourself, you know that carnivores feed especially on the old and the sick and the frail, terms that have come to cling ever more tightly to you, eroding what once was your supple skin.

But in other moments, meeting with a keen young repairman arrived to fix your telephone connection, or speaking with a knowledgeable young woman behind the counter of a pharmacy, you are pricked by a lingering optimism, and you marvel at the resilience and potential of those around you, particularly of the youth in this city, in this, the era of cities, bound by its airport and fiber-optic cables to every great metropolis, collectively forming, even if tenuously, a change-scented urban archipelago spanning not just rising Asia but the entire planet.

Mostly, however, you do not think of the city, and focus instead on events transpiring nearby, in your living room and kitchen, or on reality-warping phantasms and reveries, transported by your brain as powerfully as by any manu-factured technology, though with far less design, or on the pretty girl, with whom you settle for hours, alternating ob-servation with argument or laughter. Together you and she have discovered a passion for cards.

You sit at this instant, side to side, the person's width of sofa between you your playing table. The hands you have been dealt are held close, averted. A wrinkled finger of ash hangs from her cigarette. You lift the ashtray so she can flick it, peering carefully to see if she twists and drops her wrist. No such luck, this time.

"Cheat," she says.

"A compliment, coming from you."

Her own eyes take in your posture, the inflection with which you lower the ashtray to the sofa. You are a gifted bluffer, inscrutable, as steady with a bad hand as with a bountiful one. It is your strength. Hers is her unpredictability, her instinct to win big or lose big, to eschew the odds. It is also her weakness. And while both of you suffer from mediocre memory, what you lack in recall you jointly make up for with slow, smoldering intensity.

"I'll raise you, little boy," she says.

"Well, well. That tells me all I need to know."

"I'm sure." She arches a slender brow.

"Wait and see, pretty girl."

You call. The hand is yours. Chance, really.

You scoop the pile of what were originally backgammon chips, smooth and cool to the touch, mostly whites but a pair of blacks too, sliding them your way. She rises to fetch herself a glass of lemonade.

"It must hurt," you say.

Inwardly she seethes. But outwardly she grins. "It's not over yet."

Returned to the sofa, her drink on her armrest, she examines you as you shuffle. Your gaze is focused, like a mechanic disassembling an engine, with none of that cloudiness that can descend upon you so suddenly. She leans forward and waits. You notice. You kiss.

When the pretty girl's death comes it is mercifully swift, at diagnosis her cancer having spread from her pancreas throughout her body. Her doctor is surprised that she is in so good a superficial state. He gives her three months, but she lasts only half that, refusing to relinquish smoking until the very end, when breathing itself becomes difficult. There is no point admitting her to a hospital, and so she spends her final weeks at home, cared for by a nurse, her factotum, and of course you, who tries to hunt down her favorite movies for her to watch an ultimate time. Never fond of prolonged cuddling, she leans against you now, and allows you to stroke her sparse white hair, though whether she does this to comfort you or to be comforted, you are not entirely sure.

"I don't want you to be alone," she tells you one afternoon, as you sip your tea.

"I won't be," you say. You attempt to add that her factotum is here, and her tenant, and on the telephone your son. But you are unable to form the words.

Medications do not relieve her pain, but they make it less central, and in her center builds instead a desire to detach. It costs her to be touched, as she approaches her finish, companionship softly irritating her, like the remaining strand of flesh binding a loose milk tooth to its jaw. An almost biological urge to depart is upon her, a birthing urge, and at the end it is only with great consideration for what has been, with love, in other words, that she manages to look up from her labors to give you a smile or squeeze your hand.

She dies on a windy morning with her eyes open. You arrange to bury her at a graveyard belonging to her community. She might not have had much to do with them, but it is unclear to you where else she ought to be buried. Besides a preacher, a pair of grave diggers, and a prospecting band of professional mourners, who tear up and moan with robust commitment, there are just three of you in attendance.

The actress who was the pretty girl's tenant sticks around for a while, because the pretty girl has asked her to, but uncomfortable in a house otherwise occupied only by men, and despite the low rent, eventually she departs. The factotum stays, in part out of loyalty to the pretty girl and in part because it is easy to skim money from you. You do not begrudge him this. You would do the same. You have done the same. It is a poor person's right. Instead you are grateful for his help, for his refusal to sever you from your few remaining possessions by violence. The townhouse's water pressure has dipped so low that filling your tub takes an eternity, and therefore you must be sponged, sitting naked on a plastic stool in your bathroom and unleashing the occasional prodigious fart, and this the factotum does for you twice a week, without complaint.

Until one day you wake up in a hospital bed, attached to interfaces electrical, gaseous, and liquid. Your ex-wife and son are there, and they look a little too young, and you have

a moment of panic, as though you have never left the hospital, as though the last half decade of your life were merely a
fantasy, but then the pretty girl enters. She too is a little too
young, and maybe she has just heard of your heart attack
and rushed here from her home in the city by the sea. But it
does not matter now. She is here. And she comes to you, and
she does not speak, and the others do not notice her, and she
takes your hand, and you ready yourself to die, eyes open,
aware this is all an illusion, a last aroma cast up by the
chemical stew that is your brain, which will soon cease to
function, and there will be nothing, and you are ready, ready
to die well, ready to die like a man, like a woman, like a
human, for despite all else you have loved, you have loved
your father and your mother and your brother and your sister and your son and, yes, your ex-wife, and you have loved
the pretty girl, you have been beyond yourself, and so you
have courage, and you have dignity, and you have calmness
in the face of terror, and awe, and the pretty girl holds your
hand, and you contain her, and this book, and me writing it,
and I too contain you, who may not yet even be born, you
inside me inside you, though not in a creepy way, and so may
you, may I, may we, so may all of us confront the end.